HUNT FOR JUSTICE

Book One:
A BOUNTY EARNED

James R. Vernon

A Three Moons Realm Novel

Table of Contents

Just a few people that deserve a special thanks.

My immediate family for supporting all of the time and effort I've put into this journey.

My editor, Josephine Hao, for constantly teaching me new ways to ale my writing better.

My excellent beta reader, C.D. Verhoff, for helping me shake off the bad habits of a new writer. I am becoming an adequate adverb killer and plot steamliner thanks to her help.

My cover artist, Daniel Kamarudin, for the amazing work he created that reflects the story and the world in the pages of the novel.

Chapter One

A Rowdy Crowd

Season of the Chill, 185 AP

Temple Bounty - 10 Silver (Alive)

Ezzy Ciantar stepped into the Last Stop Inn in search of the one man that had caused her father's death and taken away her family's livelihood. Although she had never met the man, she clutched an artist's sketch of her quarry's deceptively plain and innocent face. After two years of searching and chasing false leads, she had decided to go back to the last place he had been before her family's tragedy.

Pulling the hood of her cloak back, letting her raven hair cascade down to her shoulders, Ezzy's eyes scanned the common room for potential candidates to question. Unfortunately, the place was a crowded mess. There were too many people, too many chairs and tables crammed together, for such a modest-sized tavern. Discarded food and empty mugs littered the floor. In the back, a long bar was packed with men, the waitress or perhaps the owner, slinging drinks from behind it. Three serving girls skirted around the mostly full room, trying their best to keep up with the orders of food and drink from those at the tables. They also were trying to dodge the grabbing hands of some of the more rowdy men.

All of it made Ezzy sick.

"You know," Nolan said, limping into the room behind her, "I can ask around without you. That way you don't have to subject yourself to all of this."

"I can handle it," she replied, turning around to face him. "I've been in worse."

He stood there wearing his usual vexed expression. His shoulder-length copper hair was tied behind him. The lines and wrinkles that decorated his face made him look two generations older than Ezzy instead of two decades. His clothes always matched his mood. Tonight, the ensemble was a black coat over a navy blue shirt and black pants. In his right hand, he carried his walking stick, a simple piece of oak sanded smooth with little decoration. He scanned the room with a pained expression. Did he ever *not* wear an annoyed expression?

"Worse in terms of appearance, maybe. But we've never been in a tavern this packed this late into the night. Most of these patrons are probably a few mugs deep into their evening festivities. I don't expect they will be as cooperative in answering--"

"Nonsense. I've seen how a few drinks can loosen tongues."

"It also makes men a bit more forward. And more likely to react in a violent manner. We might have enough money to last us a while now, but it wouldn't hurt to find a job or two for Paz. That won't happen if we have a repeat of the same events that occurred in Halyquain."

Throwing her hands in the air, Ezzy let out an exaggerated sigh. "How many times do I have to apologize for that? You've repeatedly brought it up all season--"

"It happened less than six days ago--"

"--and it really wasn't my fault. I was already angry about being sent on a wild goose chase. My temper got the best of me."

"Yes, well, I would prefer to sleep in a bed instead of outside for a change. So if you could control your temper and not get us run out of this town, I would appreciate it."

"I can control my temper just fine, thank you very much. Besides, you're the one that has a problem with being around so many people--"

"Don't start with that."

"I won't, because you're going to let me get to work."

She spun with a flourish, letting the hem of her golden-colored cloak strike the man, then strode into the middle of the room. What did Nolan expect her to do when that man in Halyquain had placed his hand on her backside? Ezzy had broken only two of his fingers. It wasn't her fault that the five or six of the man's friends had decided to get involved.

And she had promised to pay back the sobbing innkeeper for all of the damage. Eventually.

Reaching into the small bag slung around her shoulder, she dug out a few pieces of paper. Each one had the same drawing inked onto it: the face of a man around Ezzy's age, with shaggy black hair and a nondescript face. It would be pure luck if anyone in the tavern remembered seeing such an average-looking young man that was part of a caravan passing through well over a year ago. It would have been helpful if Fredren had drawn her a picture of the man's sister as well, but he claimed to never have seen her and didn't even remember her name.

Risking a glance back at the door, she let out an exasperated huff at the sight of Nolan still standing there. The man worried too much. Sending him her best annoyed look, she waved him towards the other side of the room. He needed to get started if they were going to get through the whole room before the patrons were too far along in their drink to remember much of anything.

Not waiting to see if Nolan limped into the room, Ezzy turned to the closest table.

"Hello gentlemen, I was hoping I could bother you for a moment."

Out of the five men sitting at the table, the one closest to her, was the only one to look up from his mug.

"Sorry lass," he slurred as his eyes tried to focus on her. "We're all farmers at this table. There is no way any of us could afford a girl that wears expensive cloaks and a fancy green dress."

"Afford? Afford what?"

Even as the words left her mouth, the meaning struck her like a whip. Her fingers curled into fists at her sides. How dare the man imply she was a prostitute?! Well, he had made it seem like she was a high-caliber prostitute, so that was something.

Wait, what was she thinking!

"For your information," she got out through clenched teeth, "I'm a member of one of the most powerful Hawkpurse families in Ven Khilada."

"That just makes you one of Drenk's whores," another man chimed in That got a laugh from the rest of the men at the table. It took all of Ezzy's willpower not to punch him in the face.

"The reason I approached your table," she said in the sweetest tone she could manage, "is that I'm looking for someone. A person that passed through here almost two years ago. He looks like this."

She held out one of the portraits, slowly passing it in front of them so that they all could see. Three of the men glanced at it for a moment before shaking their heads. A fourth didn't even bother to look, his attention wandering to a serving girl as she passed. The fifth man, the one that had originally spoken, took a long look at the paper then a longer look at her.

"You're the Ciantar girl, aren't ya," he said in a more somber tone. "I recognize the bear claw insignia on your cloak."

"Yes."

"I'm sorry lass. Your father bought from my family's farm for years. It was a shame what happened to him and your--"

"Yes, thank you," she said, cutting him off. "I'm sure my family made you lots of money. Now, if you could help me find this young man..."

The man that had called her a 'whore' stood and shook his mug at her. "No need to get all high and mighty. From what I hear, your family--"

"It's ok, Meryl," the first man said, placing a restraining hand on the man's arm. He waited until Meryl sat back down before returning his attention to Ezzy.

"I remember that day your father's caravan came through. There was a travelers' wagon with the rest of the trade caravan heading into the Deadlands, but I never saw any of the people riding in it."

"Do you know someone that might have? If it helps, I also heard his sister was traveling with him."

"Oh? You should try asking one of the waitresses. I remember one going on and on about being treated poorly by a girl with that caravan. She mentioned two men with the girl, so one could be the guy in the picture."

"Yes!" She could barely hold in her excitement. "He spent a lot of the trip with a Saniteal named Iacane. The second man could be him."

"Well, like I said. I didn't see them. Here, hold on a moment." He turned and waved at a short brunette carrying a tray full of food. "Gladdy! Come on over here, cuteness."

"In a minute, hun!" she called.

Gladdy dropped off the food she was carrying and tucked her tray under her arm before making her way over to the table. A plain girl in a loose brown dress, there was nothing to distinguish her from any of the other serving girls Ezzy had seen. Was being plain the requirement for working in a tavern or inn?

"What can I get you, Tom?" Gladdy said, flashing a friendly smile.

"Nothing for me, lass--" A few coughs from the rest of the table, made him grin. "Well, I suppose another round for me and my friends, but this lady also has a question for ya."

Gladdy turned and looked Ezzy up and down, a frown marring her features. "Yes?"

"This gentleman here, Tom, is it?" The man she had been speaking to nodded. "He said that almost two years ago, the last time the Ciantar caravan came through, you had a bad experience with a girl and two men. Do you remember them?"

"Oh yes, I remember that day. The girl and her brother arrived first, and then an older man joined them. The girl was very rude and had an air about her. Like she was better than everyone." She glanced at Ezzy's cloak for a moment before continuing.

"Her brother kept trying to get her to behave, but it was clear he had no control over her. It wasn't until the Saniteal joined them that she stopped shooting me angry looks."

"The brother, did he look like this?" Ezzy shoved the picture she was holding in the girl's face.

"Uh, yes? I didn't pay him much mind but that could have been him. I think his name was Ren? Or maybe Ben? I remember it being something short."

"Ean?"

"Yes! Ean, that sounds right."

Grabbing the waitress' arm, Ezzy pulled her close. "What else do you remember? Did they say where they were from? Where they were going after they left the Deadlands? Did they ever pass back through here?"

"I...uh...don't remember much else. I never saw them again. The Saniteal's name was Iacane, if that helps. They all seemed pretty chummy."

"I know that. No one knows where Iacane is either," Ezzy mumbled to herself. Doing her best to control the frustration she felt, she released the girl's arm. "Do you remember anything else? Even the smallest bit of information might help."

"Not about that Ean fellow, but the Saniteal did pass through here again."

"What?"

"The Saniteal. The one named Iacane. He passed back through--"

"Yes, I know. I heard what you said." The shock of finally finding new information had caught her off guard. "Did you talk to him? Do you know where he went next? Were Ean and his sister with him?"

"I just saw him go into the town Healer's shop. Didn't talk to him. You should ask Joseph Traint. It was his shop. He might remember the man."

"Great. Is he here?"

"No, he stays with the Yanst family most nights. Their son came down with a horrible cough. Strangest thing, since his family has always been--"

"Yes wonderful, he is helping some sick boy. Where is this family's home?"

"You're not thinking of going now, are you?" Gladdy asked.

"You can't go bothering that family this late at night," Tom chimed. "Their boy needs rest."

"It's really important that I talk to this man. Every day wasted is a day I fall farther behind."

"Then you'll just have to make it up some other way," Tom said in a way that made it clear he considered the conversation over. "Joseph will be in his shop tomorrow morning. You can talk to him then."

After a year of knowing nothing and then following too many rumors and wild goose chases the past few seasons, to be this close to something tangible and have to wait was too much.

"It's really not that late, after all only one of the moons is up. I could just stop by for a moment, get the answers I need, and then be on my way."

Tom shooed Gladdy away before turning in his chair so that he was facing Ezzy. Whatever he had had to drink that night must have run its course, as he was looking at her with eyes that were both sober and intense.

"Listen girl. I understand what happened to your family was horrible--"

"You have no IDEA what my family--" she tried to cut in, but he spoke right over her.

"--and not one of us will ever know what it's like to have so much and then lose it all. But if you're looking for this young man, this Ean fellow, because you believe he was the one responsible, you need to let it go. Revenge can ruin a person, and your family has already been through enough."

"Let it go?" she growled, "Let it go?! This 'young fellow' is the reason my father is dead. The reason my mother and two younger brothers are forced to live in a shack they can barely all fit in. He is the reason that the other Hawkpurse families were able to steal everything from us."

Two years of pain and frustration bubbled to the surface.

"Let it go? I'll let it go when Ean is brought to justice or buried in the ground."

"Listen, lass, from what I heard of the whole affair, the few survivors all have mixed versions of what happened in the Deadlands. I've heard stories about strange magics. Many said the Living Dead that call that land their home are always looking for a reason to start trouble. I've even heard that it was your father that started the whole massacre—"

He cut off as Ezzy's fist connected with his jaw.

The blow rocked him out of his chair, and he fell over onto his side. Ezzy was bent over looking him in the face before his eyes regained their focus.

"Don't you ever talk poorly about my father again! Do you hear me?"

Tom nodded, although Ezzy wasn't positive he comprehended what had happened yet. His friends unfortunately did. All four of them were on their feet, their chairs pushed back and each wearing matching scowls. Ezzy glanced them over and didn't find a single reason to worry. The four stocky men were sure to be strong from years of hard labor in the field, but farmers seldom had formal training in the art of combat. When the one closest to her took a step in her direction, she rose from Tom's side and stuck her palm out at him.

"This is a bad idea. I'm not looking for a fight, but I won't shy away from one either."

"No one cares what you are looking for," the closest one slurred, "but you won't get away with hitting my cousin."

He tried to throw a clumsy punch in her direction.

She caught the man's wrist with both hands. Using momentum, she spun him around and yanked the man's arm up and behind his body. He let out a yell before she released his wrist and grabbed his hair in one smooth motion, then slammed his head down onto the table. His face hit the thick wood with a crunch, and she released him as he slumped to the floor.

Ezzy straightened and prepared herself for the next attack, but instead of finding three more men rushing her she found them staring at their fallen friend.

"I'm going to go now." She tossed a few silvers on the table. "Here. For tonight. When your friend wakes up you can get him drunk enough to forget what happened, and there is enough that you can join him."

"You think you can pay us off with a few drinks," one of the men growled. "Why don't you take those coins and shove them up your dead daddy's arse."

The knife was in her hand before she even realized it. She was about to lunge when something struck her across the stomach. It wasn't a hard blow, but there was enough force behind it to stop her in her tracks. Looking down, she found Nolan's thick oak walking stick resting against her belly.

"I think it's time for us to go." His tone was one Ezzy recognized well. He used it often when she was younger and mistreating her toys. Even now she felt the desire to listen, but what the man had said...

"I'm not about to let these buffoons insult my father without putting them in their place." Her voice was calm and controlled, but her muscles ached with the effort not to lunge at the man.

"Didn't you mention something about being able to control your temper?"

"Yes, but this is about defending my father's honor."

"He wouldn't want you to defend it by killing a drunken moron."

The drunk in question took another step towards them both. Before he could take his second step, Nolan swung his cane around, placing its tip right in the man's face.

"Don't say a word. I'm trying to save your life here."

The man stopped, which disappointed Ezzy. She had hoped he would ignore the warning and come at her. If he had, everyone in that tavern would have learned why you don't disparage the Ciantar family name.

"Ezzy," Nolan placed his free hand on her shoulder. "Can we go?"

She let out a grunt and replaced the knife in its sheath at her waist. Nolan was right. Her father would not approve of bar fights and killing drunks. He would have walked away, and that was exactly what she was going to do. Well...

In one smooth motion Ezzy grabbed a stool and swung it at the man.

She hadn't put a lot of force behind it, but the stool caught the man in the chin and rocketed him backwards. He hit the ground without uttering a sound, his arms and legs spread out in every direction. The remaining men at the table stared at their fallen friend with wide eyes and gaping mouths. The other patrons at the inn began to laugh at the fallen drunk. Most of them did, at least. Those that didn't find the situation funny were staring at her with nothing but animosity.

And there were enough of them to make even Ezzy worry.

"Time to go," she said, patting Nolan on the back as she moved towards the door.

"We passed that point," he murmured in reply but followed along after her.

They left the inn, stepping out on the main street. The few lit lanterns did little Even the one moon that should have been up at this point in the night was absent, its light hidden behind a now cloudy sky. Waving Nolan to follow her, she moved past two alleyways and took a left down a third. She chose this alley without a nearby lantern as the best place to watch the inn's entrance. If anyone was coming out after her, she wanted to be ready.

Nolan limped along after her. When he reached the alley he pushed past her and leaned against the wall of the building.

"Wonderful. You know there is only one other inn in this sewer of a town. Deep in some of the worst sections--"

"Quiet," she whispered in a harsh tone. He mumbled something under his breath but grew silent.

He was right of course. Wethrintir was a sewer.

One of the older towns in Ven Khilada, Wethrinter looked as if one of the gods had taken a wheelbarrow full of houses and dumped them out, letting them stay wherever they landed. The complete chaos of tightly packed buildings created a rat's nest of alleyways that went off in multiple directions, often ending suddenly. It was easy to get lost in this town once you were off the main street and was just as easy to disappear in it. That was why over a decade ago, the town had been overrun by an army of bandits, raiders, and thieves who held it for almost a year. It took an army led by one of the strongest Heroes to finally free it from the scum of the land. Every last villain was driven out by the Hero, Yaland the Fist, restoring the town to its former innocence.

At least, that's what the stories said.

As the daughter of one of the most influential men in all of Ven Khilada, Ezzy knew differently. It was impossible to drive all of the scum out of this labyrinth. Main Street was like a shiny butterfly that distracted you from all of the maggots living deep inside the town.

And now Ezzy had killed any chance of them staying in one of the few safe places in and around Wethrintir. Well, she would make it up to Nolan at the next town or village they visited. Probably.

Standing in the shadows, Ezzy watched the door, hoping that the friends of the drunk didn't come out looking for her.

"How long do we have to wait?" Nolan whispered in her ear. He had moved closer to try to see around her.

"Until I'm confident that we can leave without being followed. Now shut up "

"Leave? So we're going to camp outside of town? Great, another night of sleeping on the hard ground."

"You just said the other inn was in the worst part of town," she growled.

"Yes, but at least they have beds."

"Beds that we could get our throats slit in--"

"I don't think it's that dangerous. I'm sure at worst we would just get robbed."

"At worst? It's not like we have an unlimited supply of money any more. If we lost--"

"Hush. Someone is coming out of the inn."

Hush!

It took all of her willpower not to kick his cane out from under him. Clenching her fists to help hold in her anger, she returned her attention to the street. Sure enough, four bald men were walking out of the inn and into the light of the lanterns by the door. They looked younger than the men Ezzy had gotten into a confrontation with, and they were all dressed in similar dark green shirts and maroon pants. Each man also wore an orange headband around their bald heads. With a dismissive wave of her hand, Ezzy rounded on Nolan.

"Now listen here, I will not be hushed--"

"Esmerelda! Quiet!"

The combination of his tone and his use of her full name got her attention. She gave him a questioning look, and he pointed back towards the street.

"I think those gentlemen are going to be more trouble than the drunks you angered inside."

Ezzy watched as the three men made some sort of hand signal towards the other side of the street. A moment later, seven more men wearing similar colored clothes walked out from various alleyways and joined them. They started talking amongst themselves, with one man pointing directly to where Ezzy and Nolan were hiding.

"Lookouts." Nolan said, lightly grabbing her arm. "We need to go. Now."

"Agreed."

Moving as fast as Nolan's bad knee would allow, they hurried down the confining paths between the buildings. The alleys really were a maze, and as they took random turns left and right, Ezzy lost all sense of direction. With barely enough room for the two of them to walk comfortably shoulder to shoulder, she felt like the walls were closing in on her. It also didn't help that the alleys were devoid of any lanterns. They couldn't even rely on light coming from a window--all of the buildings were windowless. More than once they walked straight into a wall when the alley branched off suddenly.

After their seventh turn down an alley that looked the same as every other one, Ezzy called for a halt. They had to have lost the men by now. They had taken turns at random and bypassed other alleys. It might take them all night to find a way out, but at least they were safe.

"Do you really think it's a smart idea to stop?" Nolan panted, his head swinging about as he tried to watch both directions at once.

"I'm sure we're fine. I didn't see anyone following us as we moved, and it's not like their outfits would be that hard to spot." She let out a short laugh.

"This is no laughing matter. You realize, of course, those 'outfits' signal membership in one of this town's many gangs?"

"Yes, which means they are a bunch of thugs and not very bright."

"Just because they are thugs does not mean they are all idiots. I think we should keep moving before it's too late."

"It *is* too late," a voice said from above them.

Snapping her attention up, Ezzy gasped as men dressed in the garish green shirts, maroon pants, and orange headbands began to drop from the roofs of the smaller buildings on either side of them. By the time Ezzy had backed up against Nolan, fourteen men had both of the exits from the alley effectively blocked off. And each man held a blade in their hand.

"Nolan, have I ever told you I hate it when you're right?"

Chapter Two

TRAPPED IN A MAZE

"Well, at least it's not thirteen thugs," Ezzy said, trying to keep her voice calm. "That would be unlucky."

"Yes. Quite." His tone told her exactly what he thought about her observation. Nolan never could look on the bright side.

"Gentlemen," she made a slight bow towards the thugs. There was no way to tell who the leader was, so she did her best to address everyone at once. "We are hardly worth the trouble of robbing. We have little money--"

"You tossed plenty on the table at the inn," one of the men said with a laugh. She recognized him, although he had not worn the headband in the common room, and a long-coat had hid the colors that they all seemed to wear. What gave him away was that a small corner of his left nostril was missing. Hard not to notice a characteristic like that, even from across the room.

"All for show," she replied. "The coins are painted and worthless. This," she pulled at her extravagant cloak, "I stole. My companion and I were just trying to scam some money out of that table of fools. I'm sure you saw how that turned out."

She hoped the scuffle in the inn helped support her lie, but if they also thought about how she had manhandled the one drunk, all the better.

"Don't see how a hoity-toity girl from the Ciantar family would need to scam farmers for money," one of the thugs barked.

Wonderful, one had overheard the conversation.

"Even with her family business destroyed, I bet they had lots of coins hidden away," another added. "I would bet my left eye those coins were real."

"You already lost your left eye when you pissed off Bullwhip," said another.

"I know," the second man popped out a wooden eyeball and held it up. "That's why I wouldn't mind betting it."

That earned the man a round of laughter from his fellows. Ezzy might have joined in if things didn't look so grim. The fact that the men felt they could joke around was a clear sign they weren't afraid of anyone happening upon their little mugging. Ezzy and Nolan were on their own. Mostly.

"Well," she said, grimacing when her voice cracked slightly. "I'm sure we can come to an arrangement that doesn't involve any bloodshed."

"Sure, my ladyship," wooden eye gave her a mocking bow. "Hand over all your money, any jewelry you have, and come along without a fuss. You do that, we won't rough up your servant here too much."

"The money, of course, is no problem. Unfortunately, any jewelry I had was sold long ago. As for coming with you, I'm sure you understand that would be a waste. If you know my family has fallen from grace, then you must know that any ransom for me would be less than the money you would spend to keep me fed."

That caused another round of laughter.

"Ransom?" Missing nostril scoffed. "A pretty girl like you will make us a nice bit of coin working in a brothel."

"You probably couldn't afford a girl like her!" Another man shouted, sending the thugs into a roaring round of laughter again.

"You think you can turn me into a prostitute!" Nolan tried to grab her arm, but Ezzy pushed him away as she stormed over to the man. "If any man tried to even touch me without my permission, I'd snap each of his fingers!"

"Fiesty, too!" Nostril joked, sticking a stubby finger in her face. "But just like every other girl, you'll break--"

"Poor choice of words," she said in a flat tone as she snatched his finger and twisted her wrist. The accompanying crunch brought a smile on her face.

Snatching his hand back with a yelp, Nostril cradled it against his body. He retaliated with a clumsy kick that Ezzy avoided with ease. She swatted it down, causing the man to spin and tumble to the ground. He put his hands out to stop his fall, and let out a high pitched squeak as his injured finger hit the dirt.

Expecting the other men to rush to his aid, Ezzy was surprised when instead they all burst into laughter yet again.

"She got you good!"

"He'll have problems fondling his own parts now!"

"Guess he won't be picking his nose with that finger!"

The men continued to toss out their jibes until a voice cut through their laughter.

"Enough!"

A bald man stepped past the group of thugs blocking off the path. He wore the same garments as the rest of the gang, but stood a head taller and walked with a confident gait. A thick, bearded head covered in scars sat on massive shoulders. A large whip hung coiled from his waist. He moved next to Ezzy, ignoring Nolan, and glanced down at his fallen companion.

"You've disappointed me again, Trak," he said, shaking his head at the man. "Always underestimating marks. First, with that man that sliced your nose and killing three of our men, and now with this little lady."

"Bullwhip, I was just having some fun," Trak whimpered. "It's only a broken finger. I'll be fine."

"I swear, Trak, your brain has the rot. This is the last time we let you pick out the target. Matter-of-fact, I think your time with us has run its course."

"Excuse me," Ezzy cut in, "this seems to be a private affair. If you'll just let me and my companion go--"

She didn't see the blow coming.

The back of the larger man's hand caught her square in the jaw, knocking her hard against the buildings. The breath left her body and she slumped to the ground.

"I'll get to you in a moment, lass," Bullwhip said, barely turning his head to look at her. Returning his attention to his fallen man, he made a dismissive gesture towards him. "Clean this garbage off my streets. Drop him in Viper's Nest territory. They can get rid of him for us."

"Wait!" was all Trak could get out before the men gathered on his side of the alley swarmed him. They rained blows and kicks on the man until he grew silent. When he was a bloody and unconscious mess, three of the men picked him up and carried him away. That left Bullwhip, the obvious leader, and ten other men.

Still impossible odds for the two of us, Ezzy thought. Especially since she was still struggling to breathe.

"Now," Bullwhip grunted, "back to business. We have a fallen Hawkpurse and her faithful Thaljori."

Ezzy felt like she had been struck again. How did this man know Nolan was a Thaljori? The thug must have read the surprise from her face.

"Oh, I know a lot," Bullwhip said. "Unlike my former peon, I do my research. I know all about how the two of you have been traipsing around, looking for the person responsible for your family's downfall. I must say, you move pretty quickly. Last I heard you were making your way to Halyquain."

So he hadn't heard about what happened in Halyquain yet, Ezzy thought. *Good.* Bracing her back against the wall, she rose back to her feet.

"I don't know what you want with me," she said, "but I'm sure we can work something out."

"You?" He barked a laugh. "You are going to be put to work, just like that idiot said. A pretty girl like you will be a good source of coin. The real prize here is your Thaljori. The gang's power and influence will grow tenfold with him making Vilathos for us."

"I would never do such a despicable thing," Nolan said, finally stepping forward. "I wouldn't let a gang of thugs and murderers obtain that much power."

"Oh, you'll do it. If you work for me, I'll make sure she doesn't get abused too badly serving men." Bullwhip's voice dropped to a threatening tone. "If you don't, I'll let every one of my boys have a turn carving into Ms. Ciantar here. When they're done with her, I'll be lucky if I can make a few copper coins off of what's left."

"You wouldn't!" Both Ezzy and Nolan exclaimed.

"If you know anything about how things work here in Wethrintir, then you know I would." Turning his back on the two of them, Bullwhip waved a hand over his shoulder at them. "Take them both. Don't hurt the Thaljori, but be as rough as you need to be to take the Ciantar girl."

As Bullwhip disappeared around a corner, three of his men moved towards Ezzy. They walked with swagger that suggested they didn't expect much of a fight

She would show them rough.

The first thug that got close earned himself a kick to the groin. The second, a broken nose. When she landed a three punch combination that floored the third man, they started taking her seriously.

The rest of the gang members moved the fallen men out of the way and formed a tight semi-circle around Ezzy and Nolan. With their backs against the wall, they had very few options. Nolan began waving his cane about defensively, which just earned him more laughter from the thugs.

"Is help coming soon?" he asked, before nicking a gang member with the edge of his cane.

"Yes."

The thugs began to close in tighter.

"Maybe it should hurry up?"

"I thought you didn't want a repeat of Halyquain?" She kicked an overeager thug in the chest. The rest of the gang slowed their advance. "I'm trying to avoid causing a scene."

"This is much different than what happened in Halyquain. Causing a scene

———— ◆ ————

would be quite acceptable under these circumstances."

"If you say so."

A large crash echoed through the night, followed by startled yells. The noise made the thugs stop their advance.

"Did you hear that?" one asked.

"Sounded like a building collapsed."

"What could make all of that noise?" a third chimed in.

"It's trouble," Ezzy replied, flashing those around her the sweetest smile she could imagine.

Another crash sounded in the night, followed by a scream. Nolan glanced over at her.

"I'm sure it's just people getting startled. They'll be fine."

Another crash, much closer this time. The thugs started glancing around, hands going to weapons at their waists. Another crash, this one close enough that she could feel it vibrate through the walls.

"I don't like this," one of the gang members said looking around.

"Me neither."

"Should we go?"

"Stop wasting time," Wooden Eye cut in. "I'm sure none of you want to go tell Bullwhip that we lost his possessions. Just rush them, and we can get off the street."

The men turned their attention back to their prize and were about to follow through when the corner of the alleyway exploded in a shower of wood and stone. Everyone ducked down, including Nolan and Ezzy. Shaking some of the debris from her hair, she looked up at the cause of the destruction and smiled.

"There's my boy."

Leaning against what remained of the building was her Vilathos.

Standing almost as tall as the building itself, it looked humanoid in the sense that it had discernable arms, legs, body, and head. Flat slabs of iron made up its feet, with large oval pieces in place of its arms and legs. Four-fingered hands flexed as it pushed itself off of what was left of the building wall. Its body was a huge block, made of more iron than it would take to make dozens of swords. Small metal joints connected each piece and bent with the flexibility of a blade of grass. On top sat a block of metal shaped like the top of a rook chess piece, with two glowing, sky-blue gems sitting where eyes would go, and small extensions on the top of the head. All in all, it was an intimidating sight.

Except to Ezzy. To her, it was her most prized possession. Her Paz.

"Ok, gentleman," she said, 'time to play."

With a thought, she sent Paz after the men.

The ten gang members had a mixture of reactions. The smartest three, which included Wooden Eye, took off down the alley in the opposite direction. Three more of the men seemed frozen in place, either by fear or awe of her wonderful guardian. The last four, the closest to Paz, made the foolish mistake of attacking.

Swords and knives were in the thugs' hands as they leapt at the Vilathos. They hacked and slashed at its arms, legs, body, pretty much anywhere their blades could hit the large construct. They might as well have tried to chop down an old oak with their bare hands. The blades failed to even scratch the surface of the magic infused metal of Paz's body.

Unfazed, Paz ignored the weapons and attacked.

It grabbed the closest thug by the head and tossed him into the air. The man let out a yelp as he sailed over the rooftops and into the night. By the time the sound of him crashing onto a roof reached them, Paz was swinging a massive arm at the next gang member. The man ducked under the deceptively fast swing. Unfortunately the momentum of the attack kept the arm moving and it crashed through the wall of another building. Ezzy grimaced as a yell escaped from somewhere inside.

"Sorry!" she yelled.

That was a mistake. Her voice seemed to shake the three frozen men out of their stupor. They turned on her, each carrying a blade and a threatening look.

"Kill her quick!"

"Will that stop that monster?"

"Only chance we got."

The fools had been kind enough to give her warning.

They rushed her. She took two head-on, slapping a sloppy stab away from her body with one hand, then ducking a swipe aimed at her throat from a second man. Nolan did his part, tripping up the third man's legs with his cane while she moved in closer to the two men. A second shot with the cane to the thug's temple put him out of commission, just as Ezzy disarmed one of the two men attacking her.

And then a green and maroon blur crashed into all of them.

When Ezzy shook the stars from her eyes, she found herself underneath a foul smelling thug who was thankfully unconscious. She rolled the man off of her and glanced around.

The battle was over. Five of the gang members were down, the slow rise and fall of their chests showing that they were still alive. Well, six if you counted the one that Paz had launched into the air first. It was doubtful he had recovered from his landing already though. The man who had blanketed her had been one of the men foolish enough to attack Paz.

Her Vilathos was standing in the center of the alley. Its task completed, Paz waited for instructions. All around him was destruction. Four separate buildings had holes punched into their walls, along with the building at the end of the alley that was missing its corner.

"This is much worse than Halyquain," Nolan grunted from behind her. Using his cane to push up off the ground, he glanced around at the damage.

"Yes, well, you said we were in much more danger than when we were in Halyquain."

"From the walls?"

"I'll work on teaching Paz how to fight in closer quarters."

Nolan took a few pokes at the bodies around him. "You might also want to teach it not to throw the bodies of its enemies at its allies."

"Noted. When I get the chance, I'll get right to work on that."

"You can start tonight. You're going to take Paz south of town. Get as far as you can tonight and then make camp."

"But I need to talk to the Healer, what was his name, Joseph? I'm sure it's still early enough--"

"You must be kidding me!" Nolan face had turned a light shade of red and his whole body trembled. A rare sight for the usually somber man.

"Nolan, this is the first solid lead we've gotten in I don't know how long..."

Limping over, he placed a firm hand on her arm.

"Do you not see the damage around us? We are in a lot of trouble. YOU are in a lot of trouble. You need to be out of town right away. I'll stick around and talk to the Healer."

"I'm sure if we explain what happened..."

Of course at that moment one of the damaged walls completely collapsed. A lit candle cast a dim light on a living room on the other side of the destroyed wall. Peeking out from underneath a table was a woman with a young child. They both looked terrified.

"Alright," she relented, "we'll leave tonight. Are you sure it's safe for you to stay around?"

"Safe enough. Head due south and I'll meet you late tomorrow. Now get going."

"Be careful, Nolan," she said before walking over to Paz. Lifting her arms, she ordered the construct to pick her up. Grasping her in its giant hands, Paz placed her on his shoulder. Giving one last nod to Nolan, she had Paz carry her off into the night.

Chapter Three

OUTSKIRTS

Temple Bounty - 25 Silver (Alive)

Paz had carried her south late into the night. By the time they had stopped, the clouds had cleared, and all three moons hung high in the sky. Their green, blue, and red light bathed the area, creating an array of tiny rainbows in the dew that was starting to form on the grass. It really was a beautiful sight. Even Ezzy, who didn't care much for the beauty of things, had to admit it was striking.

When she found an acceptable spot to camp, she had Paz drop the oversized bag he wore on his back packed with all of their camping supplies, then sent him off to try and find some dry wood for a fire. Since it was only the beginning of the Chill season, the night wasn't painfully cold. She could survive if she needed to without a fire if she curled up underneath her blankets in her tent, but she would prefer a little warmth. Luck was not with her, though, as everything Paz brought back was too wet to light.

"Can't you tell the difference between a good stick and a bad one?" she said, shaking her finger at the construct.

Silence was all she received in return.

Ezzy knew that the Vilathos wasn't a living creature with a single thought of its own, but sometimes it made her feel better to talk to it. Especially when she was alone. She had spent more of her late teenage and young adult life with the Vilathos than with anyone else. That was probably why she had gotten so good at instilling complicated instructions in it. Nolan had said even at a young age, she was a natural Handler.

Setting the Vilathos to guard their location, Ezzy had crawled into the tent, wrapped herself up in her blankets, and fallen right to sleep last night.

Even with the uncomfortable ground and slight chill in the tent, Ezzy had been able to sleep soundly. With nothing else to do but wait, she had let herself sleep in till late morning. After rising, cleaning up the tent, having a few pieces of fruit for breakfast, and then having a one-sided conversation with Paz about the finer points of caravan management, Ezzy had run out of things to do.

Waiting was painful.

Not like the sharp pain of a wrist broken during a sparring match or the slow burn of going a few days without food, but having to wait all day on the southern plains of Wethrintir made Ezzy's entire body itch. Ezzy had always been a person of action even from a young age. She led her younger brothers around from the moment they could walk, like a shepherdess leading her flock, making sure they did what she wanted while keeping them out of trouble. When her father was away on a caravan, she controlled the house. Well, as much as her mother would let her.

Stuck out in the middle of an open field with nothing to do but sit and stare at her Vilathos, she was starting to go stir-crazy.

"This is your fault," she said as she tossed a damp stick at Paz. "If you hadn't caused so much destruction, I could have stayed to talk to the Healer. Now we have to wait."

The stick bounced off of Paz's arm. The Vilathos didn't move.

"Oh, don't you act all noble," Ezzy continued. "I've spent years training you to avoid crashing into walls. I assumed that included what you hit when you swung your fists. You turned most of those walls into windows."

Silence.

"You could at least feel a little guilty about it!"

Through their bond, she commanded Paz to raise his hands to cover its stone face. It complied, which gave it the appearance of an ashamed child. Ezzy liked it. If she got really bored she would spend some time instilling a command that would make him repeat the gesture whenever she said a few keys words. Maybe later. She was having a good time relieving some stress by admonishing an inanimate object.

"And throwing that thug at me! That was certainly the worst thing you did last night."

Paz remained hidden behind his hands.

"Oh, don't you dare turn this on me. I've taught you a wide range of fighting tactics, but unless I'm controlling every little action, you just do the same routine. Pound and throw. Tossing an enemy is only affective if it doesn't end with them on top of me."

Still Paz hid. Ezzy felt a pang of guilt for a moment, then quickly squashed it. It was one thing to have a conversation with a mindless creation, it was another thing to feel bad about berating it. She commanded Paz to lower his hands.

"Alright, alright. I can admit when I'm wrong. I put the effort in training you not to hit Nolan or me, but I never taught you anything about not throwing things in my general area. You're not at fault...this time. But I'm going to make sure to fix that problem during the trip, so don't you go thinking you can get away with it again."

She had Paz nod.

"Good. Glad we see eye-to-eye. Now, I'm going to take another nap. You make sure to keep any animals away from me and wake me as soon as Nolan returns."

Setting Paz to his guard routine, Ezzy dug out her blankets from the bags and spread them out across the grass. *Might as well get a little sun*, she thought, and stripped down to her undergarments. Paz would warn her before anyone got close enough to see more than they should. With the light breeze and clear skies, the weather was too perfect not to take advantage of the chance to lie out. The colder temperatures of the season would come soon enough, so this might be the last chance she would have to get a little color.

"Don't you judge me," she said as she lay down on the blankets. "We both know I'm not completely vain. I just don't like how pale I get during the Freeze and Thaw seasons."

She knew it was her imagination, but the creak of Paz's joints as it began its patrol almost sounded like laughter.

***

Ezzy sat up the minute Paz's guard routine stopped. Grabbing her clothes, she got dressed as fast as she could. Since Paz hadn't sent an alarm through their bond, it meant Nolan was approaching. She glanced over to find him much closer than she would have liked before she was completely dressed. The Thaljori had been around her for most of her life, but that didn't mean Ezzy was comfortable enough to be half naked in front of him. By the time the man walked up to camp, Ezzy was covered in her usual attire.

"You have good news, I hope?" she asked as he took a seat across from her.

"Why hello, Nolan," he replied with a dry tone. "Glad to see you are still alive, Nolan. Can I get you something to eat or drink, Nolan, after you limped your way out here?"

"Stop being overly dramatic. You look fine, and I bet you slept in a nice, comfy bed and had at least two good meals."

"Perhaps. But I also had to avoid people asking questions about you and the damage you caused last night."

"Technically, Paz caused it."

"Technically, you control Paz, so…"

"Whatever. Did you learn anything?"

"Yes. I learned that you angered enough people that they are petitioning to put a bounty on your head. And not just a local bounty. They are sending it to Lurthalan and Avien'zia's temple."

She flashed her biggest smile. "So pictures of my face are going to be posted up in villages and towns throughout the realm? I hope they find an artist that can properly portray my looks."

Nolan rose with a growl and moved right in Ezzy's face.

"You foolish girl! This is not a joking matter! A bounty means bounty hunters."

"Like some bounty hunter would have any chance against Paz--"

"Quiet! You think this is a joke? How are you going to track down this Ean fellow if we are dodging bounty hunters? It certainly will make it that much harder to find work for Paz. Do you have any other skills you haven't told me about that can make us more money? As much money as we save sleeping outside every town and village you get us kicked out of, we still have to buy food."

"I could take up hunting to handle the food problem..."

"And let's say we run into some bounty hunters on the road, or worse, get in a fight around other people. If you have to use Paz to protect us and more destruction occurs, what happens then?"

"Well, uh..." she tried to reply but he continued to speak right over her.

"I'll tell you what happens. Paz causes more damage, they put a bigger bounty on you and probably one on me once they realize I'm with you, and then we'll have Heroes or even worse, those fanatics of Avien'zia coming after us. We won't last a quarter of a season on the run from either of them."

"What did you want me to do!" she screamed, her resolve finally breaking down. "They were going to take us. Use my body until they couldn't get any more money out of me and then kill me. You, they would have kept you working until your mind broke from the strain of bonding Vilathos. I saved both of our lives!"

She was crying. Why was she crying? She rarely ever cried.

"Oh, Ezzy," Nolan whispered, then leaned in and wrapped his spindly arms around her.

She didn't know why, but that one action by her closest friend opened up the floodgates. Ezzy began to sob uncontrollably.

"I'm sorry," she got out between sobs. "I don't know what I'm doing anymore."

He held her tight, giving her reassuring pats on the back when the tears flowed strongest.

"I've had everything taken away from me, Nolan," she cried into his shoulder. "My father, my life. My mother and brothers struggle to get by every day. I should be home, putting what money father left me to make things better. Instead I'm dragging you all over Ven Khilada, hunting rumors in some vain attempt to find some justice. Or revenge. I don't know which it is anymore."

"It's justice, Ezzy. I wouldn't be here if it was anything other than justice. We just need to be more careful. Especially with a bounty on your head."

"Oh, Nolan." Ezzy pulled back so that she could wipe her eyes and try to gain some control over her emotions. "Mother will be so disappointed in me when those posters start going up in Lurthalan. And she'll have bounty hunters bothering her all the time."

"We'll get a letter to her when we pass through Lurthalan that explains everything. I'm sure she will understand."

"It would be better if I told her in person."

"We can't take that chance now. Word of your bounty will reach Lurthalan long before we do. If I was a bounty hunter, the very first place I would stake out would be your mother's home."

"Ugh," she grumbled, sitting back and putting her face in her hands. "You're right. As always. That must be a great feeling, to always be right."

"It's troublesome at the best of times," Nolan replied. His smile signaled that he knew her words held no ill will. 'I would avoid Lurthalan completely if we could, but we will need to get supplies, and any other settlement would take us too far out of the way."

"So, you have an idea of where this Saniteal is?" Hope perked her right up.

"Yes, the man I talked to today said that this Iacane fellow mentioned he was headed down to Shade. Something about researching the effects The Wall has on the people that live beneath it."

"That's wonderful!" Falling forward, she wrapped her arms around Nolan's neck. He struggled to keep them both from tipping over, finally succeeding after a few grunts and groans. "Well, I don't really know that much about Shade. That's the Janpair family's region after all. But it's still a great lead."

"Yes, well, it means a lot more traveling," he said, carefully detaching her arms from around his neck. Ezzy couldn't help but smile when she saw that he was blushing. The old stiff. He really was bad at handling any emotion other than irritation.

"Not a problem. We're becoming experts at roaming the land."

Rising with the help of his cane, Nolan glanced around the makeshift camp.

"Well then, expert traveler. Should we get going? There is still plenty of daylight left, and the trek to Lurthalan will take us eight or nine days on foot. Might as well get a strong start."

"Sounds like a plan. I'm looking forward to a nice, leisurely stroll across the plains to Lurthalan. Should be fun."

Grinning, Ezzy began packing up her things while Nolan worked some life into his bad knee.

Paz remained where he had last stopped, waiting for an order to move.

Chapter Four

CHANGE OF FAITH

The trip took more than eight days and it certainly was not pleasant.

Nolan had lived most of his forty-seven years without taking a single step outside of Lurthalan. He had been born there, trained there, and had all he needed in the city. When he sustained the injury to his knee, he rarely took two steps out of his own home. He relied completely on his Vilathos back in those days for everything: cooking, cleaning, taking his orders to the shops to be filled--his Vilathos had done it all. Now, he was out limping around the countryside, fighting off thugs, and on a hunt for a single man in a great, big world. The irony of it all was almost funny.

Almost.

On the second night of their trip, a fierce thunderstorm descended upon them while they slept. Sitting out on the plains, they had nothing to protect them from the elements except their flimsy tents. The combination of the wind and heavy rain assaulted them worse than the gang had in Wethrintir. At one point, he thought the gale was going to carry him off, tent and all. He pictured his slim frame tumbling around the inside of the tent while the winds flung him into the Deadlands, or even worse, the lands of the Shadaer Umdaer. Needless to say, he was still awake when the storm moved on and the sun began to rise.

Ezzy, of course, loved the whole experience. That morning, as they ate cold rations on a wet ground, all she could talk about was the storm.

"It was like I could feel every raindrop as it hit the tent," she mumbled with a mouth half-full of fruit. "Back in our old home, I used to sit in the observatory during a big storm and listen to the downpour, but to actually feel it..."

Nolan nodded as Ezzy relived the night. He always enjoyed watching Ezzy's excitement as she experienced things for the first time.

To say she had been sheltered most of her life was a huge understatement. Private tutors, self-defense trainers, Sparktellers to entertain her and her younger brothers, and the occasional Vilathos toy that Nolan made for her were the only outside interactions she received. Her father kept her locked up more tightly than his fortune.

As the oldest child in the family, Ezzy had been trained from birth to take over the family business. Her time was spent learning about trade routes, the other Hawkpurse families, and everything she could fit in her head about the land. This left little time for the rest of the world. Everything had been viewed out of the many windows of her home, seen through the illusions of a Sparkteller, or read about in books. Now she got to experience everything the world had to offer, and she was drinking it in with a wild exuberance.

"I didn't want to sleep, it was so exciting," she continued. "Unfortunately, the beats of the rain were soooo soothing I fell asleep."

"Yes, most unfortunate."

"Do you think it will snow?"

"What?"

"Snow. I've never been out in the snow before. Do you think it will snow sometime soon? It's cold enough, right?"

"No, it rarely snows this season. And if it does, it's usually at the end of the season, not now at the beginning."

"Hmmm," she mumbled, her mind probably wandering off to something new. As soon as they finished their breakfast, they set out.

During both the fifth and sixth days, another storm decided to take up residence directly above them. After waiting out the entire first day in their tents, they had a choice to make on the second day: brave the weather and push on or stay huddled in their tents and hope the storm blew over.

Loving the storm and not wanting to soak her expensive clothes, Ezzy decided that they would stay put. As night fell and the storm raged on, she made a mad scramble out of her tent and into Nolan's tent.

"I was getting bored", she said, shaking the water out of her hair and spraying him in the face.

"Still a fan of storms?"

"Not so much anymore. Do they usually last this long?"

"Not usually."

"Think one of the gods is angry at us?"

The question caught him by surprise. Since her father's death and the downfall of her family, Ezzy had cut off all effort to worship any of the gods. She had gone as far as to curse out Drenks, her family's patron god, on multiple occasions and had cursed Nolan out as well the one time he had told her to stop. Being the wise man that he was, he never brought up religion again in front of her. For that same reason, Nolan decided to tread carefully here.

"I'm sure it's just a regular storm."

"But what if it's not? What if Drenks has finally decided to pay me back for all of the horrible things I say about him every day?"

"I'm sure he would understand after what you've been through. Plus, it's GanZroe that influences the seasons and the weather. Have you been saying inappropriate things about them?"

"No."

"Well then, nothing to worry about. I'm sure the weather is no more mystical than the dirt we've been sitting on."

"I guess."

Leaning forward, he placed a hand on Ezzy's shoulder.

"Alright, out with it," he said. "You've been educated about the gods more than I have. What do you really want to ask me?"

"It's annoying how well you know me." Leaning back on her elbows in the small confines of the tent, she let out an exaggerated sigh before continuing. "Nolan, which deity do you worship? I mean, which one do you mainly worship? I know we are supposed to send prayers to all of them, but which one do you lean more towards?"

"Why do you ask? You know that can be a very personal question to ask someone."

"Oh, and we're not close enough for me to ask personal questions?" She lightly kicked his arm with a soggy boot.

"You've never asked me a personal question in the past."

"We've never been stuck in a tent for two days in a row."

"Ezzy..."

"Fine, fine. I do have my reasons, but one of those reasons is that I want to know you better. You've been working with my family since before I was born, and the only things I really know are your name, that you've lived in Lurthalan all of your life, and that I trust you like family."

Nolan could feel the heat rising in his cheeks from the compliment. Trusting him as much as a family member was more than Nolan had ever received from anyone else in his life. He had never wanted a family of his own, preferring solitude over companionship. Most Thaljori lived this way, especially with the way long-term use of their type of magic messed with the mind. But if he had wanted a family, and a child to call his own, he would have wanted her to be exactly like Ezzy. Strong-willed, curious, ambitious, charismatic. Pretty much everything he wasn't. The fact that she trusted him so completely warmed his heart.

"Ni'Aren." he said. "The goddess of wisdom and knowledge."

"Really?" She sounded disappointed. "She's ok, I guess. Why her?"

"I've always been curious about how things work. Especially once I realized I had the ability to be a Thaljori. I have performed hundreds of bonds over the years, and I still don't understand half of what I do. It's all instinct, and that can be quite stressful considering the possible dark consequences when things go wrong."

"That makes sense...I suppose."

He shot her an annoyed look. "Alright then. How about you? It's obvious you have moved on from Drenks. Has anyone taken his spot in your mind?"

"Yes."

Finally, the point of the entire conversation. "Well? Who is it?"

"Avien'zia." She said the name in a hushed tone.

"The goddess of the hunt?" That certainly was surprising. "Why?"

"To help us, of course! We haven't exactly had the best of luck so far. Finding out where to find this Iacane fellow has been our first big break in the past year. If he is still in Shade, of course. If that lead runs dry, we'll be out of options. Divine intervention would be our only hope at that point. Plus, I think a strong *female* deity is just what I need in my life right now."

"Understandable."

"That's it? That's all I get? *Understandable.* I just opened up about a major decision I've made for my life!"

"Well, I'll say one thing about it."

"Yes?"

"If you get on her good side, maybe she will mislead the bounty hunters."

"You are impossible!" she said, letting out a frustrated scream that rivaled the wind and rain outside in intensity. "Fine. Make jokes when I open up to you and keep bringing up my mistakes all in the same sentence. I don't care."

"Ezzy, I was just saying--"

"I'm tired," she said, grabbing one of his blankets and rolling onto her side. "I'm going to try and get some sleep."

"You're staying here?"

"You don't expect me to scramble back to my tent in a downpour, do you?"

He thought about mentioning how it was her idea to come to his tent in the first place, but decided against it. Best not to add fuel to the fire. Maybe having her nearby would help him sleep better while a war of the weather happened just outside. Probably not, but the thought gave him a little bit of hope.

"No, you stay here. Just try not to kick me too often in your sleep."

"I will make no such promise," was the last thing she said to him as they curled up for the night.

***

She had kicked him a total of eleven times that night, four of which he knew were intentional. It wasn't until her breathing became regular and the kicks were more dream spasms than the result of her anger that he realized she was asleep. As much as he cared about the girl, she was hard to understand. Sometimes she joked right along with his dry sense of humor and other times, like tonight, she took even the slightest comment as a personal attack. It had made their journey so far a tense affair.

The storm let up in the middle of the night, and they got moving at first light. Ezzy did her usual routine after a fight of not talking to him the first part of the day. Then, probably getting bored, she started speaking to him as if nothing had happened the night before. That was why Nolan never worried that much about their little spats. Ezzy was quick to forgive and forget.

They traveled on without incident for the next couple of days, stopping for each meal and enjoying the perfect weather that followed behind a storm. It was a peaceful trip during those days. Very little wildlife roamed the plains between Wethrintir and Lurthalan. They saw the occasional rodent or small prairie dog, and the occasional bird of prey, but for the most part, the only sights were small, rolling green hills. It made Nolan rethink his desire to live in the busy city he had always called home. Maybe he would enjoy retiring to the solitude of the untamed lands of Ven Khilada. Once he had finished helping Ezzy, of course.

The peaceful days had to end eventually. On the ninth day, with the sun high in the sky, they crested a hill and found the first of the many farms that littered the countryside outside of Lurthalan. Most of the land directly around the city was owned and operated by the various Hawkpurse families, while the farms on the furthest outskirts were owned by families not associated with anyone else. The farm in front of them was modest; a small barn, main house, and a few worker homes sat on the other side of three fields, each field full of the season's last harvest of corn. A few people were moving about the stalks, blurs of movement hidden by the tightly packed plants.

"Should we go down?" Ezzy asked, placing a hand over her eyes to block the sun. "I could go for a nice, home-cooked meal."

"Not all farm families are friendly. Especially those that don't have the support of one of the Hawkpurse Families."

"Still, we could at least try."

"Or we could keep going and be that much closer to Lurthalan, where there are plenty of places to eat home-cooked meals. Places with nice soft beds and places to bathe."

"Fine, fine. I get your point. We keep going."

Ezzy usually put up more of a fight over anything they disagreed on. Not wanting to question one of the few times he won an argument, Nolan let it go without another word.

They traveled the rest of the day. The further they went, the more farms they came across, the land getting more and more packed with fields, pastures, and barns. The workers on the farms all stopped their chores whenever they passed. Ezzy's Vilathos always drew a lot of attention.

It wasn't that Vilathos were rare. There were many in the realm; most large trade caravans made use of them. A large supply were used in the mining town of

Harlyquain, dozens were created for construction and personal use in Lurthalan, and the largest one ever created worked in the Rensen sawmill. But it was rare to see a small group traveling with one out in the countryside. So, the farmers stopped and gawked at the construct, while Ezzy grinned and enjoyed the attention.

Nolan on the other hand did not like it one bit. They stuck out like a Taruun in a group of children. The storms might have slowed down word of Ezzy's bounty just as it had slowed them down. Or someone might have gotten word out on pigeons and her face was plastered all over Lurthalan already. He would only relax once Ezzy hid Paz somewhere when they got closer to the city. And then only a little.

They camped for the night, rose early, and before the sun had risen very far in the sky, they rounded a hill and Lurthalan came into view.

"Finally," Ezzy said with a laugh. "Civilization."

"That's one word for it.'

"Bah, you are such a grump. Let's go. If we hurry, we can be in the city before nightfall. One of the inns has a bath with my name on it."

The thought of a warm bath to ease his aching joints was enough to improve Nolan's mood. As Ezzy picked up the pace, he did his best to limp along after her. They might be in for a world of trouble in the city, but Nolan would face anything that life threw at him if he got a few moments to sooth his sore body in a nice, hot bath first.

Chapter Five

COMING HOME

Lurthalan.

The only settlement in the realm large enough to be called a city. Divided in half by the Melcoi River, Lurthalan sat on the southern edge of the Great Melcoi Lake. The west side contained most of the buildings: the docks, a few of the temples, the Water Market, Merchant's Circle and hundreds of homes. The east side of the river held mostly temples, the Hero's Refuge, and a solitary inn. Two roads led out of the southern end of the city, one on each side of the river. A stone wall began to ring the tightly packed buildings on the west side of the river, its construction started a few years ago. Built by Vilathos twice Paz's size, the wall was dwarfed only by the temples that spotted the city landscape. Massive structures completed before the time of the Plague, the temples were each unique and a sight to behold. Hundreds of followers gathered both inside and outside of each temple every day or crossed over the Melcoi Bridge from one side to another.

Which Nolan believed might be a problem.

The temple of Avien'zia sat just outside the western gate. A huge circular building made of wood and furs, it was often surrounded by the casual devotees of the goddess. Small tents, cooking fires, tanning racks, and anything else associated with hunters littered the grounds. Shouts filled the air and blood stained the earth. All the massive temple of Avien'zia and surrounding tents were missing in order to be included as a district of the city was a name. The majority of people that lived in those tents were hunters, butchers, and leatherworkers, which was of no real concern. It was the other men and women, the ones in garishly decorated leather armor and carrying a plethora of weapons, that made him worry.

Bounty hunters and Fara'korin, the elite trackers of Avien'zia, swaggered among the tents and makeshift stalls. The Fara'korin had no equal when it came to hunting men and were expert marksmen. They wouldn't be a problem though. Avien'zia's special hunters took too much pride in themselves to take any notice of Ezzy. Whatever small bounty she had on her was nowhere near enough to catch their interest. Ezzy could hold up a wanted poster with her face on it to one of the Fara'korin and they would laugh at her. They would probably tell her to become more interesting as well.

It was the regular bounty hunters that Nolan worried about. With no moral code, little to no compassion, and an appalling lack of basic hygiene, they would turn over their own mother for a few coins. If word of Ezzy's bounty had already reached Lurthalan, most of the bounty hunters gathered around the temple would have a picture of her in their possession. If that was the case, their only hope was that her bounty was small enough that it wasn't worth memorizing for most of those gathered in the area.

Approaching the city, Ezzy had Paz drop their bags and then sent it to sit amongst the other Vilathos constructing the wall. It wouldn't look out of place there, even with his unique, all-metal design. It would also keep Paz close, just in case they needed him.

With Paz out of the way, the two of them blended into the mass of people walking into and out of the city, and got as far into the middle of the crowd as they could. It was close to mid-day, which worked out well for them. The roads into the city were packed this time of day. People and carts jostled as they moved about, the crowd pushing in on them like grapes caught in a wine press.

He had forgotten how horrible it all was. He hated being touched since he had been a child, so it was almost painful to have so many people rubbing against him. His stomach began to churn, his vision blur. The people, so many people, all around him...

Something slid into his hand. He glanced down and found a small, tan hand in his, squeezing gently. Looking back up, he found Ezzy studying him with compassionate eyes.

"It's going to be ok," she mouthed to him.

He focused all of his attention on that hand. Felt the pressure she applied. Let the crowd around them disappear. His breath returned, his stomach calmed. Closing his eyes to the world, he let Ezzy lead him through the crowd.

How his anxiety over crowds of people had gotten so bad, he didn't know. He hadn't been around many people during his training. Years of keeping to himself after he went out on his own and only coming out to perform jobs had made the problem more acute. The physical attack he suffered that gave him his limp certainly played a large role as well. But he had always felt nervous and on edge around large groups of people, even at a young age. Having lived in the city his entire life, he should have learned how to manage it.

Instead he was struggling just to put one foot in front of the other and was being pulled through the crowd like a child. He should be keeping watch. They were probably passing Avien'zia's temple this very moment. He should be scanning the crowd, looking for any signs of recognition on the faces around them. A normal man or woman was just as likely to give them away and collect part of the reward as a bounty hunter. Nolan felt utterly useless.

Blind to what was going on around him, he stumbled through the crowd. At one point, Ezzy picked up speed, pulling him faster than before. Fearing trouble, he risked opening his eyes. A sea of men and women surrounded him. A rainbow of different colored clothes assaulted his eyes, increasing the sense of disorientation. He lost his focus for a moment and the clamor of too many people washed over him like a tidal wave. His feet went numb, and his palm began to slip from his walking stick. When his toe hit a loose stone in the road, he almost went down, but Ezzy kept a good grip and he stayed on his feet. Shutting his eyes again, he decided it was better to be guided. Ezzy was smart enough to pick out anyone dangerous.

After walking for what seemed like an eternity, Nolan was pulled off to the left, perpendicular to the direction they had been headed. Fewer people bumped into him as they moved, until he didn't feel anyone around them at all. Only then did he chance another look.

"Are you alright?" Ezzy asked, her voice raised to be heard over the nearby crowd. She still kept a tight hold on his hand.

"Yes, yes," he got out between long breathes, "just a little overwhelmed. Give me a moment."

"Of course."

Letting go of his hand, she took a few steps further down the street. Nolan risked one glance back at the river of people as it shuffled up and down the main road, shuddering at the mass of bodies moving about. They had barely made it past the main gate. Ezzy had taken them down the first street on the left side. His street.

"I figured you might want to go home for a bit," Ezzy said. "Get some new clothes, maybe take a bath. We can meet at the High Horse for some dinner later and plan our trip to Shade."

"And what will you be doing?"

"Going to get some supplies. Maybe talk to the few allies my family has left. Try to learn what's been going on while we were away. Figure out if word of my bounty has reached here yet. See how much I'm worth." She winked at him.

"Just be careful. Don't go around boasting about having a bounty on your head."

"Yeah, yeah."

"And remember what I told you. Do not go home, even if you think the bounty hasn't reached here yet."

"We'll see!"

"Ezzy!"

Before he could get another word out, she dashed into the crowd. He only kept sight of her for a moment, and then she was swallowed by the herd of people.

Nolan let out a sigh. She knew there was no way he could manage his way up the main street after her, not with that large crowd. Well, it was out of his hands now. He would just have to hope that those smarts kept her out of trouble. And that her temper didn't get her into more of it. With nothing else to do, Nolan began to limp home.

His street was peaceful compared to Main Street. Rows of homes ran along the right side while the city wall rose on the left. Many had complained that the wall blocked their view of the surrounding lands, but Nolan didn't mind. It was funny to think that just a year ago, most of that wall had barely been started. Now, it ran along the road, past his home, and curved around the other buildings almost to the lake. An impressive piece of work, as were the massive Vilathos that were building it.

Nolan would never risk bonding anything that big. And he couldn't comprehend the strain that bonding the massive one in Rensen could have on the mind. Although, he would like to see it someday. Paz was as large of a Vilathos as he was comfortable bonding to a human, and it was a battle every time he reinforced Ezzy's bond to the metal construct. Just thinking about it made him tired.

A nap. That's what he really needed. A few moments of sleep without a downpour keeping him awake or Ezzy kicking him in her sleep. His house was perfect for sleep. No windows, few lights. Just complete darkness in his oversized bed, buried under his thick, expensive comforters. It would be heaven, especially compared to the past nights of traveling and the ones waiting for them. Just the thought made him quicken his pace.

He reached his door moments later. It was indistinguishable from the ones on either side, except for its lack of windows. With a contented sigh, Nolan twisted the key into the lock of his door and walked into his sanctuary.

Chapter Six

REST AND RELAXATION

Bliss. That's the only way Nolan could describe it. Pure bliss. Waking up in his own bed, wrapped in his blankets and in complete darkness, was the most amazing feeling. The absence of light in his room mirrored his dreamless sleep. Thaljori never dreamed for some reason. Emptiness seemed to be the theme of his life.

Except for Ezzy, of course.

Sitting up, Nolan tried to rub the sleep from his eyes. He was supposed to meet her for dinner. What time of day was it? No way to tell in his home. He had the windows removed when he moved in. When he needed his rest after a Bonding, even the slightest ray of light sneaking past a curtain would wake him. Of course with a windowless house, he could only guess the time of day if he went outside, but he had never had to keep to a schedule before so it didn't matter. People waited for him, not the other way around. Except now he wasn't being hired to do a job, he was helping the daughter of a good friend. Or was he simply helping a friend? Nolan had never defined what Ezzy was to him. Regardless, he needed to figure out if he was late for his meeting with her.

But his bed was comfortable...

"Light," he grumbled.

A large glass bowl, suspended from the ceiling in the middle of the room by a copper chain, began to glow as the flame inside burst to life. The Glowglobe was easily the most expensive object in his house, and that included his room-sized swampsilk rug from Shade. One of four installed in his home, the source of unlimited light was a product forged by an inventive pair of magic users. Inventive and rich. The convenience of the item mixed with the dangerous process to produce them increased the value of Glowglobes ten-fold. It took a skilled Elementalist willing to give away some of his power for as long as a year depending on the size of the globe, combined with an Instiller willing to risk manipulating the Elementalist's fire magic to create a Glowglobe. By now the original inventors were probably making almost as much as he had made as the Thaljori to a Hawkpurse family.

He pushed the thought and tinge of jealousy aside and got out of bed. He needed to finish packing. And he still had no idea if he was late or early in meeting

Ezzy. Nolan moved to his wardrobe first, kicking his travel bag aside from where he had tossed it before climbing into bed last night.

It still must be early enough that Ezzy hadn't started to worry about him. He could get his packing done and be all set to go, just in case they needed to make a hasty retreat. Maybe he could even get a cup of tea while he packed. He sent the order to his Vilathos to brew a cup and bring it to him.

Nothing.

He didn't have a Vilathos.

Massaging his temples with both hands, Nolan tried to clear the fog that had crept into his thoughts. How long had it been since he had control over a Vilathos? Eight years? Nine?

"Just a simple mistake," he mumbled. "Force of habit after decades of having a Vilathos of my own."

Just an excuse.

"It's being home, that's what made me think I still had a Vilathos."

You are getting worse.

"Poor sleep and having my thoughts escape me every now and then is something that happens to everyone. It's not a big deal."

Fool.

Ignoring his own thoughts, Nolan finished packing and limped his way downstairs. It was his age that muddied his thoughts. Forty-some odd years would muddle any mind a little. It was his age, and sleeping in poor conditions for so many nights. That was all. Maybe he could convince Ezzy to stick around one more night. She could sleep at his house for safety and he could get one more night in his bed.

Walking outside, he was surprised to see the sun still up, although it had mostly set behind the mountains far to the west. Surprised and happy. This late in the day meant most people had closed up their shop or had finished their work for the day, and most importantly, had already made their way home. Walking back to the main street, he found it devoid of much activity. The occasional cart rolled on by, a few hunters coming in late from their hunt, the last couple of stragglers returning with their shopping for the day. It was nice and peaceful, just the way Nolan liked it.

He let a small smile touch his lips as he made his way down the street. The High Horse Inn was farther down the main road, across from the wagon fields that sat at the beginning of Merchant's Circle. One of three inns in the city, the High Horse was by far the nicest. With the most rooms and the largest common room, the High Horse also had the best food and entertainment every night. While most of the clientele had a great deal of money, it wasn't uncommon to see the occasional fisherman, hunter, or tradesman at the bar. The owners didn't discriminate; if you had the money, you were welcome in the High Horse. And when your money ran out, you were expected to leave and make room for the next paying costumer.

Even before he reached the bottom of the porch that wrapped around the front of the inn, he could hear the sounds of merriment and music drifting out of the front doors. The one guard standing at the door gave him a quick look and nod as he walked inside. If a Sparkteller was performing, there would be a couple of guards at the doors and a line growing down the street. One guard meant some music, maybe a performer or simple story teller, but best of all, it meant a smaller crowd.

Nolan scanned the tables and bar at the back for Ezzy but came up empty. *I'm here first?* Unexpected, but she could be unpredictable at the best of times. Unless she got herself in trouble...

He let out a laugh and moved to an empty table with the least amount of patrons nearby. If Ezzy got herself in trouble, he would have seen or heard about the destruction. She was probably just making some last minute preparations. Definitely hoping that they would leave tonight.

When a waitress stopped by his table, he ordered some bread and a glass of alcohol-free cider. If he was going to convince Ezzy to stay in the city for one more night, he would need his wits about him.

Leaning back in his chair, Nolan glanced around as he waited for his food. At the other tables sat finely dressed men and women wearing the colors of Hawkpurse families, mingled about with a few hunters still covered in specks of blood, and a variety of other people of indeterminable profession. And there were a few of the Taruun, of course. Towering men and women with marble-colored skin and sharp edges to their features where most people had curves. The Taruun only worked with trees, either foresters or woodcrafters for the most part. They stood out in most villages and towns, but were a common resident here in Lurthalan. On the stage, a man played a lute, another a drum, and a woman sang the familiar songs of hard work and enjoying life. At the bar sat more of the working class, smiths covered in soot and burnt clothes, carvers with a thin layer of sawdust in their hair, and a few farmers still in their overalls. It was interesting to see all of the different classes mingling about. The common room of the High Horse was one of the few places in the realm where people talked freely with one another across the class divide.

His attention returned to his own table when the waitress returned with his order. The smell of the freshly baked bread made his stomach growl, and he quickly paid for his meal and tore a piece off to eat. The bread was soft and warm and had a slight honey taste to it. With a contented sigh, Nolan sat back and waited for Ezzy to arrive.

***

Three mugs of cider and another half loaf of bread later, Ezzy still hadn't walked through the doors. Night had descended over Lurthalan, and the common room was starting to get packed. The patrons that had been here since Nolan arrived were starting to get a little sloppy as well. One man had already been tossed out for falling over a table, and Nolan had to wave off a woman that tried to sit at his table and start up a slurred conversation with him. People began to jostle his table and chair as they moved about. Nolan's breath started to catch in his throat as he felt the crowd pushing in on him. Ezzy needed to get here soon.

When a patron spilled his mug onto Nolan's table, splashing him with what smelled like burnbeer, he decided to go get some air outside. He pushed his way through the crowd, using his staff to herd the drunks out of his way. His stomach churned with each person he bumped against until he finally stumbled through the swinging double doors.

A cool breeze washed over him as he made his way to the porch railing. Sweat dripped from his brow. Leaning a little over the side, Nolan did his best to keep down the bread and cider. The state of his mind might be up for discussion, but the stress and sickness that came about whenever he was in an overly crowded area was getting worse.

"Pull yourself together," he whispered to the cold night air.

Taking a few deep, calming breaths, he slowly began to feel better. His stomach settled and he felt himself ease back from the verge of passing out.

"You ok, buddy?"

The deep-set voice made him jump. Feeling foolish, Nolan turned around and nodded at the guard.

"Yes, yes. I'm fine. Just a little woozy is all."

"Alright. Maybe you should take a break from drinking for a bit then."

"Yes, I think I'll take that advice. Thank you."

With a shrug, the guard took up his post by the door, leaving Nolan alone again with his thoughts.

I hope this lead finally gets us on the right track. I don't know how much longer I can traipse around the realm and place myself in situations where I'm surrounded by people.

Nolan was smart enough to know that his years of self-isolation were the main cause for his anxiety around crowds. He wasn't a Healer or a Saniteal, but he knew enough to recognize his problems were partially self-inflicted.

At least their next destination, Shade, was a relatively small town. Built underneath the Unyielding Wall, Shade was supposed to be a tight-knit community. Rumors about the people who lived there ranged from funny to strange, and all had some connection to the Unyielding Wall. No one knew when the wall had gone up or who built it, but it predated the Plague. And it was magical. The rumors said that whatever magic was used to make it was bleeding out into the surrounding land. Which included the animals and people in Shade.

The village of Shade was run by the Janpair family of the Hawkpurses, as opposed to Ezzy's family, the Ciantars. They had been the ones to fund the settling of the town, and held an iron grip on the land. Not one of the stronger families, they were still feared because of their erratic behavior. The easiest way to Shade would be to pay for passage on a Janpair trade caravan, but with Ezzy's history and how well-known she was amongst the other Families, they had a better chance of having Drenks himself carry them to Shade than getting the Janpair family to allow them passage. With Paz having to carry their supplies, the only option they had was to continue traveling by foot. They'd cross over Melcoi bridge in the heart of the city, leave through the east gate, then travel south through the Coriana forest. They would reach Shade in a few dozen days. With any luck, they would find better weather on this trip.

Probably not, though.

With a grunt, Nolan pushed himself up off the porch rail. No point in putting himself in a bad mood before they had even departed. After all, his goal for the night was to convince Ezzy to stay in the city. One more night in his own bed would be pure bliss. It was just a matter of convincing her that--

"Hurry up!" a voice said from a little bit down the road. Nolan squinted as he tried to make out where the voices were coming from. With only the green moon out so far and the street lamps spaced out, it took him a few moments to spot the two forms moving towards the inn. They walked with hurried steps, the shorter of the two struggling to keep up with the long strides of the second, taller man.

"We don't even know if Zeke and Dean are at the High Horse," the shorter man said. "We should just go back and collect the bounty ourselves."

"The post said she was dangerous."

"Not dangerous enough to warrant even a gold coin. It's just one girl after all."

"All that means is she hasn't done enough yet to warrant a large bounty--"

"It's not even an average-sized bounty--"

"There haven't been many bounties posted in a while. We need to take whatever we can get."

"It would be enough to help get us through the cold season if we split it only two ways. I told you we shouldn't have spent so much money on that Soushade armor."

"Enough, Danny," the taller man barked. They had reached the stairs of the porch and were walking up. "We look for Zeke and Dean inside. If they aren't there, then we swing back to Fisher's Row and try to take the girl ourselves. That a fair enough compromise?"

"Yeah, I suppose that's fine, Ben."

"Good, 'cause that's what we were going to do anyway."

Nolan waited until the two had passed inside then limped down the stairs.

Foolish girl!

Of course the men could have been speaking about some other bounty. Some other girl. But Ezzy's mother and two younger brothers lived in one of the small shacks that littered the area on either side of Fisher's Row. Add to that the little comment she said before leaving his company earlier, and it had to be her. Nolan needed to warn her before things got bad--for her or for whoever tried to capture her. Like the man said, her bounty at the moment was small, but if a fight ensued and she brought in Paz for help, he couldn't see any way where a dozen of the shoddy houses in the area wouldn't get destroyed in the ensuing chaos.

Fisher's Row wasn't much further down the street from the High Horse Inn, but he had no idea how much time he had to get there. How long would the two men spend looking for their buddies? Did they know exactly where Ezzy was? Or had they just seen her go into the maze of shanties and shacks? Too many questions and his blasted knee made it impossible for him to even walk at a brisk pace.

As he approached the edge of Fisher's Row, the sounds of activity increased. Almost its own little village, Fisher's Row was made up of orphans, vagabonds, simple fishermen, and anyone else that had lost or been driven from their homes elsewhere. The buildings themselves reflected their occupants; mismatches of used boards, stone, and whatever else people could find, mashed together to form what could barely be called a house. Most were built into each other, some even leaning on other buildings, creating a maze that rivaled the alleys in Wethrintir.

Thankfully, Nolan knew exactly where to go.

Chapter Seven

HELLO AND GOODBYE

"How could you have done something stupid enough to get a bounty placed on your head?"

Ezzy had only seen her mother Alexia this angry twice before in her life. The first time had been when she had convinced her brothers to swim out to the middle of Lake Melcoi. All three of them had almost drowned and had to be saved by a local fisherman. The second time was when she had initially been bound to Paz. The two had come to blows that day with her mother being the victor. By the burning look in her mother's amber eyes, they might come to blows today as well.

Ezzy, her mother Alexia, and her two brothers Max and Mox, were all gathered in the one large room that was both their living room and bedroom. A small stove sat in the center of the room with four cots lying in each of the corners. Max and Mox, ages twelve and eight, were both sitting on Max's bed. Despite the age difference, her brothers were similar in appearance--slight of build, with spindly legs, shaggy brown hair, and bright mischievous hazel eyes. Both worked with their mother in one of the fisheries down by the docks and were starting to put a little muscle on their thin frames. Mox, who had been much smaller than his older brother just a year ago, had sprouted up while Ezzy had been away. It pained her a little to be missing chunks of their youth.

"I was just defending myself! I didn't mean to cause any damage to the town."

"We both know *you* didn't cause the damage. It was that abysmal Vilathos you keep around. I should have knocked more sense into you the first time Nolan bonded you to that thing. Nolan's lucky he didn't receive the same."

The way Ezzy remembered it, poor Nolan had received more than a few blows himself.

"We were surrounded by gang members. Having Paz help was the only option we had!"

"Gang members?" her brother Mox chimed in. "Are they like the gangs here?"

"I wouldn't call the groups of beggars and thieves that live in Fisher's Row gangs," her other brother Max replied. "They get beat up more often than they get money from anyone. It was probably the same with whoever attacked Ezzy. I bet it was just one guy that was flirting with her, and she got so scared Paz had to come and save her."

"Shut it, you little imp." She threw an empty wooden cup at Max, who snatched it out of the air. Placing it on his head, he stuck out his tongue at her.

"Don't call me an imp, you mudfish," Max responded. "I'm not the one getting into trouble."

"Oh really? So I didn't see you sneaking a mug of burnbeer from your boss down at the Old Sea Hag Inn last year?"

"You snitch!"

"Enough!" Alexia roared, her long, black braided hair whipping about behind her. "Now is not the time for bickering!"

"Sorry," all three said in unison.

"Now, back to this bounty."

"I swear, Mother. It was either I used Paz to save me and Nolan, or our lives were as good as forfeit."

"I suppose I have to take your word for it since I wasn't there. And how much is this bounty?"

"Twenty-five silver pieces," Max jumped in.

"Is that enough to turn her in ourselves?" Mox asked.

"Nah, "Max replied, "think of Ezzy as an investment. She is sure to get into some kind of trouble and bump the bounty up. Best if we wait until she reaches her full potential."

"Why you little pieces of--" Ezzy fumed, but her mother cut her off.

"The two of you. Out. NOW."

"But mom," they both whined in unison. They leapt to their feet, however, when Alexia grabbed a large, wooden spoon. Ezzy's mom caught them both once with the spoon on their backsides as they sprinted out the door. She watched them go, the faintest smile touching her lips. When they were gone, she rounded on Ezzy. For a moment Ezzy thought she was going to use the spoon on her too.

"As for you," Alexia said, brandishing the spoon at her. "I want you to stop running all over the place. I still know enough people that we might be able to get rid of this bounty IF you keep a low profile for a while."

"Mother, you know I can't do that. I can't sit here in this house when I know that the person that put us here is still out there somewhere."

"Esmerelda, you can't keep blaming one man for what happened to us. Out of all of the people that worked to destroy this family, from what I've heard, this Ean fellow was just in the wrong place at the wrong time."

"From what you've heard?" Ezzy had to clench her fists to hold in the anger that was bubbling up inside her. "I talked to someone that was there! Fredren Prown told me that it was this Ean fellow that started everything. Ean started a riot using some kind of magic."

"Ezzy..."

"I'm going to find him and make him tell me the truth, mother. If he was hired to sabotage father, after I bring him to justice, I'll go after whoever hired him. I won't stop until everyone responsible for father's death and everything that's happened to us since are brought to justice."

"And justice is bringing in those responsible for the Heroes to judge, right?"

"Yes, yes, of course. I might have Paz give them a few extra bruises, but the point is to have them brought down and locked away for the rest of their lives. Whether it's one of the other Hawkpurse families or just Ean."

"Just be careful, Ezzy. I don't want you getting so wrapped up in finding justice that you forget to live your own life. And especially don't want you to do something you'll regret."

"Oh Mother, you make it sound like I'm going to turn into some psycho. I just want to make father proud, and I know that he wouldn't be proud of me if I went around murdering people."

"I'm sure destroying buildings isn't making him happy in the afterlife either," she said, a slight smile touching her lips.

"Oh really? I heard about the one time father crashed a wagon into the Darkdwellers storage house just because the Talon of the family insulted his coat."

Alexia couldn't hold back a laugh. "Yes, well, that was during your father's younger years."

"These *are* my younger years."

"Exactly! You have the same temper as your father."

"I take that as a compliment."

Throwing her hands in the air in mock frustration, Alexia looked to the ceiling.

"Oh Drenks, why did you curse me twice. Once with a stubborn husband, and now with an equally stubborn daughter."

"Mother," Ezzy said, her voice growing cold, "I've told you I never want to hear that god's name even mentioned around--"

She was cut off as the door banged open behind her, sending a shiver through the pieced-together home. Nolan stepped in, his face pale and his breaths coming in short pants.

"Nolan!" Ezzy grimaced. How late was it? "I'm sorry, I lost track of--"

"We have to go. Bounty hunters are coming."

Ezzy blinked a few times, trying to gather her thoughts.

"How many?" she finally got out.

"I saw two, but they were going to get two more, I think."

"And they know where I live?"

"I'm not sure. They mentioned coming to Fisher's Row but didn't mention anything about your mother's house."

"Either way, it's only a matter of time until they figure it out. Let's go."

Thankfully their camping supplies were still with Paz, and she had repacked her personal bag as soon as she got home. Snatching it up from beside her bed, she was about to head out the door when her mom grabbed her shoulder.

"You can at least say goodbye. I never know when I'm going to see you again."

Ezzy's heart hurt as she noticed a single tear roll down her mother's cheek. Wrapping her arms around her mother, Ezzy gave her the biggest hug she could handle.

"I promise to send word when and if I can."

"Where are you going next?"

"Shade."

"Ezzy," Nolan cut in. "We have to go."

"One more second!" Alexia grabbed a piece of paper from one of the stands in the room and began writing something. When she was finished, she pressed the crumpled up paper into Ezzy's hand. "When you get to Shade, look for a woman named Syla Trane. She was loyal to our family, at least before everything went to the Abyss, and owns a small blacksmith's shop. Hopefully she'll be able point you in the right direction."

"Thanks, Mother," Ezzy gave her one last hug before heading out the door. It was painful only getting a few moments with her family before running off again. The fact that she didn't get to say goodbye to her brothers was downright devastating. Being gone from her family for long stretches of time was the only thing that made her rethink her quest for the man who took her family down. But in the end, her desire for justice always won out.

Nolan was standing in the alleyways that snaked through Fisher's Row when she walked outside. Still looking winded. How fast had he moved on that lame leg?

"We have to swing by my house to get my things," he said, looking around as if he expected the bounty hunters to appear at any moment.

"That's fine. We'll cut around Merchant's Circle and follow the road all the way around the west edges of town back to your house. If the hunters are coming straight from the High Horse, we will miss them completely."

Nolan nodded and gestured with his cane for her to lead. He might know how to get to her family's new home from the main street, but he had no idea how to find one of the dozen other exits out of these slums that didn't lead in the direction of the inn.

Moving at as fast a pace as she thought Nolan could handle, Ezzy began to navigate the dark alleyways through Fisher's Row. After spending a year living with her mother, she was confident in her ability to navigate the twists and turns created by the haphazardly arranged houses. The alleys here were nowhere near as intimidating as the ones in Wethrintir; the shabby homes here did little to hold in the sounds of those inside. It was almost soothing compared to the silence she had experienced passing through Wethrintir. Even so, at any time, they could turn a corner and run into someone. The only solace she found as she hurried along was the thought that Ean would eventually feel the same way as she got closer to catching him.

Turning a corner, she poked her head out and looked around. Perfect. She was exactly where she hoped to be. To her left, far down the open street, she could make out the High Horse Inn across from the wagon fields. They were on the far west side of the homes of of Fisher's Row. Across the street sat homes that were a marked contrast to the house where her family now lived. Stone and brick buildings, most two stories tall, lined the street. Towering behind them stood the temple of Drenks, a huge, oval building covered in banners of gold and silver. Flags ringed the walls of the building close to the clay-tiled roof. Each flag, sitting motionless in the moonlight, bore the sigil of a Hawkpurse family. All of the family flags were displayed sequentially, repeated four times around the perimeter of the building.

Ezzy's body shook as she looked at the four empty spaces where a flag was noticeably missing. Her family's flag. A part of her wanted to have Paz try and rip the entire building down.

"Focus," Nolan said from behind her. The foolish man knew her too well.

"This way," she snapped.

They followed the empty street towards the west side of town, then continued several more blocks into an area with multiple homes being constructed. Past that were a few more houses, some finished and others still being constructed. Then they reached an area where open space sat on either side of the road. Not even the base of the wall had been started this far north in the city, so they had a clear view of the fields and farms to the west. Far to the north, Ezzy could just make out the dilapidated temple of Iaradune, the fallen god of battle. To the south, the road curved around until homes started to pop up on the left and the partially constructed city wall sat on the right. This was Nolan's street.

As they walked towards his home, Nolan tapped her on the back.

"Don't you think you should bring Paz over? This is close to where you left him."

"Yeah, well, after I left you, I sent him over the bridge. He's sitting by the Lost Soul's Inn."

"Really? That was a smart move."

"Don't sound so surprised."

"Don't act so surprisingly responsible and I won't act surprised."

Ezzy grunted at him and picked up the pace. *Let's see him crack jokes as he tries to keep up.*

By the time they reached Nolan's home, he was sweating. Ezzy smirked as he moved past her and unlocked his door. He went in and was back out in an instant with his bag around his shoulder. When he struggled to situate the bag and lock the door, a pang of guilt struck Ezzy in the chest.

"Here," she said, grabbing the strap of his bag. "Let me take that. I can carry both bags."

"I'm fine," he snapped back at her.

"Just give me your bag, Nolan. If we have to run, you'll pass out before you even make it a few paces."

"Alright," she said after getting both of their bags adjusted on her shoulders. "Up Main Street, then over the bridge."

"Ezzy, they could be on Main Street, especially if they searched Fisher's Row and came up empty."

"I know what you are about to say and the answer is no."

"It will be safer if we cut across Main Street and head down Melcoi's Curve--"

"No, Nolan, I can't handle that."

"Would you rather risk getting caught, or worse, starting a fight and someone getting hurt?"

She responded to his question with silence. It was one thing to know he was right, another matter altogether to say it out loud.

It's fine. It's only a road after all.

If only she could believe her own thoughts.

"Let's go." She had tried to keep the quiver out of her voice and failed. Nolan looked like he was about to say something, but she spun and walked away before he could. If she was going to head down Melcoi's Curve, the last thing she needed was Nolan trying to comfort her.

Ezzy glanced back once to make sure Nolan was following her and then continued on at a fast pace. Best to get this over with and get out of town. She could handle a walk down memory lane. A very fast walk. A sprint, if Nolan could keep up.

Before she knew it, Ezzy was crossing over Main Street. The houses on Melcoi's Curve were grand displays of the owner's wealth, most of them belonging to the lower members of the Hawkpurse clans or merchants with connections to them. Cut stone and brick took the place of painted logs and planks. Slate and clay tiles covered the homes instead of thatch and wood. Grand windows adorned each floor, framed by ornate shutters and small flower boxes. Each home had extra space out front for a yard, although many were filled with flowers or vegetable gardens.

Nolan walked beside her, his attention straight ahead. Of all of the people in the world, Nolan best understood what her family had been through. He walked beside her in silence, offering neither his hand nor words of wisdom, but Ezzy didn't mind. His stoic presence alone had always given her a sense of comfort.

Melcoi's Curve got its name from the fact that it arced from east to north as it ran alongside the Melcoi River as it flowed south. The homes on the right side of the street backed up to the river, most having small beaches or decorated shores. As the two came to where the street curved, Ezzy stopped.

There, sitting on one of the largest plots of land in the city, were the burnt ruins of her family home.

Chapter Eight

A MOONLIGHT STROLL

The charred remains of the home she had grown up in looked like a skeleton left to rot. Wooden beams stuck out of the ground like the fingers of a half-buried hand. The flower beds of what had been the most magnificent garden in the city - better even than the famed garden around Ni'Aren's temple - were now piles of ash. The metal fence, with its ornate designs, had been knocked over and reduced to twisted mounds of iron. Even the cobblestone path leading up to the house had been ripped apart. It had been close to a year since the loss of her father and destruction of her family's businesses. One of the Hawkpurse families owned the property now, but she didn't know which one. But the way they had left the home destroyed, it was obvious they were trying to send a message--the Ciantar family was dead and gone.

But Ezzy would show them that it took more than that to eliminate the oldest Hawkpurse family in the realm. As long as she had breath in her lungs, she'd make the enemies of her family pay.

Starting with Ean Sangrave.

"We should go," Nolan said, causing Ezzy to jump.

"Yes, yes," she said, brushing away an unwanted teardrop. "We should keep moving."

As they followed the road, she kept her eyes on the river to the right. She needed to focus. This wasn't some casual stroll at night. They had bounty hunters after them. After glancing at her destroyed home one more time, Ezzy was starting to feel that a fight wouldn't be a bad thing. Maybe running into one or two bounty hunters would be a good thing.

"Beating up a bunch of thugs will not help our situation," Nolan said.

Could the blasted man read minds? He certainly had touched hers enough in creating the bond to Paz.

"I don't want to fight anyone," she lied.

"That's not what your expression is saying. You have the same look that you get when you're about to teach one of your brothers a lesson."

Good, he couldn't read minds. She was just really transparent. She needed to work on that.

"Beating the stuffing out of a few dirty bounty hunters would make me feel a lot better."

Nolan let out a loud sigh. "We don't need the bounty increasing just to make you feel better."

"The bounty on me."

"Don't even try to play the victim. It's only a matter of time before I'm added on to that bounty or have one of my own."

"Yeah, yeah, alright. I'll calm down. Now stop making so much noise. Do you want the whole city to know where we are?"

Nolan shook with frustration, but kept silent.

They continued up the road, remaining quiet and scanning the streets for any sign of life. This time of night it was rare to see anyone out and about. All three moons hung high in the sky, bathing the streets in their green, blue, and red glow. Ezzy found her gaze wandering to the river as the different colors danced along the surface of the water. Funny how she had never noticed how beautiful it looked growing up, when she had lived only a few paces away. Now, while she was on the run, Ezzy felt a little sadness creeping in, thinking about how she couldn't sit and appreciate the swirling reflection of colors. Of course, the mammoth building sitting on the opposite shore made it hard to enjoy the sights.

The Endless Tombs towered over every building along the shoreline, including the building connected to its left side: the Temple of Kaz'ren. The temple by itself was an impressive marble structure, but the Tombs were the second largest creation in the world, second only to the Unyielding Wall. Created by Kaz'ren herself, the black stone building stretched high into the sky and was said to stretch even further deep underground. The bodies of every single person whose soul had been claimed by Kaz'ren was laid to rest in those tombs. Even those who died before the Plague.

Ezzy's father wasn't entombed there. His body was still lost in the Deadlands. Who knew what the freaks living up there had done with him. The Soulbearers didn't travel into those lands to release a person's spirit back to Kaz'ren. Her father's spirit was stuck there in his corpse, never to be freed to return to his family. It was just another log fueling the fire of her anger towards those that had brought her family down. But again, she couldn't dwell on that now. She needed to focus on the here and now and get out of the city.

The streets were still empty when they finally reached Melcoi Bridge. Built from bone-colored stones, the massive construction spanned the river where it flowed from Lake Melcoi. The bridge rose high into the air, leaving enough clearance for the largest river boats to pass underneath. The incline was so great that if you stood on one end, you couldn't see over the rise to the other side. Ezzy's father had said it had taken the hardiest Vilathos and the most skilled Elementalists to construct the bridge.

Ezzy and Nolan both took one last look around before stepping off the road and onto the bridge. Normally bustling with activity during the day, the bridge felt barren and ominous at night. The only sounds to be heard were water lapping against the stone supports. Old stories of creatures from the Abyss hiding under bridges to ensnare their prey leapt into her mind for a moment before she squashed them. She was too old to be scared by such tales. The gods protected the city from the Abyss anyway, so there was nothing to worry about. Even so, Ezzy found her gaze wandering back to the Temple of Kaz'ren as they moved across the bridge.

How long had it been since she had prayed to the goddess of the soul and afterlife? Probably just as long as it had been since she had given her last prayer to Drenks. Did the gods and goddesses even notice when a single person stopped paying their respects? The Voices, the title given to the highest priest in each of the temples, said the gods noticed, but Ezzy was skeptical of what even the Voices knew anymore. With everything that had happened to her family, it was hard to believe in anything that came from the temples. She would continue to pray to the goddess of the hunt though. Just in case.

A hand on her arm brought Ezzy out of her thoughts. They had already reached the peak of the bridge? She glanced over at Nolan, who in turn nodded ahead of them.

Standing on the east end of the bridge were four men. They were dressed in mismatched, multicolored clothing that made each man look unique in a rag-tag sort of way. At first Ezzy thought they might just be beggars. In the low light of the moons it was difficult to make out much more detail from this distance.

The moons' light glinted off something metallic in each man's hand.

"Thieves?" she whispered.

"Could be. I can't imagine anyone else out at this time at night looking like that."

"What if they are bounty hunters?"

"I don't think it matters either way," Nolan said as he gestured towards the men. One of the four was pointing directly at them. A moment later, the men started crossing the bridge.

"What's the plan," Ezzy asked, moving closer to Nolan. "Fight or flight?"

He tapped his walking stick against the bridge a few times. "I don't think flight is ever much of an option for me."

"Well, maybe you can talk our way out of this then. These four don't look like the brightest flames in the fireplace Nolan."

"Depends on if they are simple thieves or bounty hunters. Either way, if I'm talking, you need to keep quiet."

"Why?"

"'Cause your voice always seems to enrage these types of people."

"And what types of people would those be, Nolan?"

"The awake kind."

"No need to be rude. You could have just said I'm not the best ambassador."

"I thought I did."

"Yes, true, but..."

"Shhhh."

Ezzy's mouth snapped shut as the four men drew close. Where Ezzy had originally thought they were wearing mismatched pieces of clothing, they actually wore pieces of armor that were so worn out and falling apart that they gave the appearance of being separate pieces. The men themselves looked just as worn out as the protection they were wearing. Bruises and ugly scars covered bald heads and faces that held no sign of compassion. Even their blades were nicked and look dull, although they were clean enough to reflect the moon light.

"You two out for a nice romantic walk?" one of the men said to Nolan. He had a cross-shaped scar on his right cheek. "Good for you chap, snagging a younger woman."

"We are most certainly not--" Ezzy began, but cut off as Nolan cleared his throat.

"Yes, thank you." Nolan replied once Ezzy stopped speaking. "We thought we would take a quick stroll to the gardens of Ni'Aren. Find a nice secluded spot."

Nolan actually winked at the man. If those thugs didn't each have a blade in their hands, Ezzy would have kicked Nolan right in the shin.

"Well," cross-scar said with a chuckle, "we certainly don't want to keep you from your fun. We'll just be collecting the night toll for crossing the bridge, and you can be on your way."

"Night toll? Can't say I've heard of that before."

"Oh yeah? You must not have been in the city for a while. My friends and I have been collecting here for quite some time."

"And the money goes toward the maintenance of the bridge?"

"Yes, of course. It goes towards the import of new stone and applying mortar to weakening sections, as well as--ha, oh hell. This is getting boring. Clearly we aren't tax collectors, just like from the looks of the bags you are carrying you two are not off to rub against each other in the garden. So let's just get right to the point where you hand us enough money to make us happy so that we don't have to rough you up. We ain't the most refined of fighters, and if you resist you could end up dead and we will still take everything on you."

"A fair enough deal. We're not traveling with much more than clothes and a little food, but would five silver pieces for each of you be enough to let us pass?"

"Well, that's a little low, but luckily for you, a nice fat merchant had a bit too much to drink and wandered across the bridge earlier. I thought the fool man was going to wet himself when we grabbed him. He had quite the heavy purse, enough that we'll be able to eat well for a while. Your money can go towards our retirement funds and some nicer equipment."

"Now wait a minute," Ezzy growled, taking a step towards the men. "If you don't need our money, why--"

Nolan lifted his walking stick to block her path. She gave him her meanest stare, but the look he returned made her quiet down and step back.

"Yes," Nolan said, giving her one last meaningful look before returning his attention to the thieves. "If you are going to be toll collectors, you should look a bit more respectable."

That earned a laugh from cross-scar.

"True enough! Well, how about we finish our business transaction and we can all be on our way. It's getting late and I could sure go for--"

Cross-scar cut off what he was saying and raised his weapon. His three companions followed suit.

"Hold on a moment," Nolan said, raising his hands in a calming manner. "We agreed to pay you. No need to--"

"Shut up," Cross-scar said, then gestured past him towards the other side of the bridge.

Nolan and Ezzy swung their heads around. Walking up the other side of the bridge were four more men dressed much better than the four robbing them. Well-made leather armor covered most of their bodies, the Soushade family brand decorating each. From her training, Ezzy knew that meant it was the thicker and more expensive leather imported from the Shadaer Umdaer lands to the south. Similar to the thieves, each of these newcomers also had at least one weapon in hand. Ezzy's hopes rose as the four approached. They could be part of the town guard or even caravan guards for the Soushade family. Maybe she wouldn't have to give up any money tonight after all.

Nolan looked less than thrilled.

"Two of them are the bounty hunters I saw earlier," he said with a grimace.

Without pause, Ezzy sent a thought to Paz. *Come, follow road* was all she had to say, and through their bond, Paz would find her.

Chapter Nine

PARTY ON THE BRIDGE

Nolan knew that the night was about to go downhill quickly.

"Hello, gentlemen," cross-scar said as the bounty hunters approached. "We're just concluding some business here."

One of the bounty hunters, the taller man named Ben who Nolan saw earlier, glanced at Ezzy first, and let his gaze wander over the four thieves. He smirked.

"This one is ours," he said, gesturing towards Ezzy. "I don't care about the other one. Step aside and let us take her, then you can 'conclude your business' with the man."

The three other thieves tensed, but the thief in charge kept his cool.

"Our business," Cross-scar said, "involves whichever of these two is carrying their coin purse. So how about you let us finish and *then* you take the girl."

"This girl has a bounty on her. I intend to bring her in and take whatever possessions she might have. That includes the money she has on her. Now, step aside before you get in over your head."

"A bounty, you say?" The thief glanced at Ezzy and licked his lips. "Well, that certainly is interesting. Sorry to disappoint you, but we found her first. The bounty and her possessions are ours. Why don't the four of you take your fancy armor down to the nearest inn and try to impress the local wenches. 'Cause I'll tell you right now, it don't impress me very much."

This was not going well at all. Nolan began to take a few slow steps towards Ezzy while the thief and bounty hunter continued to exchange words.

"I don't need to impress you, river rat," Ben scoffed. "I also don't need to waste my time warning you to stay out of our way. I'm attempting to save myself the hassle of killing you first and then having to hunt down the girl when she most likely flees during the fight."

"Well then, I guess to the winner goes the spoils, as me and my men aren't about to back down."

"So be it." Ben gestured towards both Nolan and Ezzy with his sword. "The two of you stand off to the side. If you try and run, I swear, *when* I catch you, I'll tan your hides so badly before I bring you in that you won't be able to sit for the rest of the season."

Ezzy of course made the mature gesture of sticking out her tongue at the man as Nolan pulled her towards the side of the bridge.

"Now that our prize is on hold," the leader of the thieves said, "let's see who the better men are."

That was the only warning the man gave before his pack of thugs charged at the bounty hunters. The two groups met with the clash of steel on steel. Men grunted as they blocked blows. Dry mortar and stone were kicked up into the air as the men jockeyed for position. The sound of battle echoed off the bridge and over the water below.

Nolan was surprised to see that the two groups looked evenly matched when it came to skill with a weapon. His first impression of the thieves had been that they were a simple pack of thugs whose decaying armor matched their fighting abilities. But these men were holding their own against the bounty hunters. The thieves wielded their blades like seasoned men, parrying thrusts and performing combinations that Nolan wouldn't expect from common thugs. The thieves must have had training from somewhere, maybe ex-city guards or even former bounty hunters themselves. At the beginning of the melee, it looked like either side could come out on top.

Training can only take a warrior so far, though. Equipment plays a large part, especially in a battle between equally skilled individuals, and the bounty hunters' gear was far superior. Their blades looked better maintained and more importantly, their Soushade armor kept them better protected. The blades of the thieves couldn't penetrate the thick leather armor. Even the heaviest slashes couldn't cut completely through, and piercing stabs only succeeded in pushing the bounty hunters back. As the battle progressed, Nolan couldn't see a single bloody scratch on any of the bounty hunters.

The same couldn't be said for the thieves. Dark red stains bloomed in various places on each of their clothing. The bounty hunters were getting progressively better at finding the weak areas of the thieves' armor or striking areas not protected by anything other than cloth. One of the thieves was already starting to show signs of fatigue, either from the battle or from the multiple dark stains that painted his clothes. It didn't look like the fight was going to last much longer,

The first man to fall though wasn't the heavily wounded thief. The lead thief, with the cross-shaped scar, lunged at Ben's neck--one of the few unprotected parts on his body. The strike missed and left the thief wide open. The bounty hunter slid his own blade into the chest of the thief with one swift stroke. A sickening gurgle was the only sound that escaped Cross-scar's mouth as the thief collapsed onto the blade. The bounty hunter shouldered the man off his weapon and wiped his sword on the dying man's body, spraying droplets of blood onto the bridge.

The loss of their leader dampened the will to fight in the other three thieves. They disengaged and raised their hands into the air.

"Enough!" one of the men yelled. "We surrender."

"We was just following orders," another said as he tossed his weapon to the ground.

The three bounty hunters looked to the man named Ben. He gave them a nod. The well-trained men lowered their swords, although they still seemed tense and ready to act.

"The three of you need to leave," Ben said to the thieves. "Now."

The words were barely out of his mouth when the thieves started running west. Ben watched them go with a smirk, then rounded on Ezzy and Nolan.

"You two certainly don't seem worth the small bounty placed on you. The old man can barely get around, and you," he gestured at Ezzy, "look a little too fancy to be much of a fighter. And the bounty is just on you, girl?"

"Send the rest of your goons away," Ezzy retorted, "and I'll show you how much of a fighter I am."

That got a laugh out of Ben and his followers. And a sigh from Nolan.

"Well, you may have the clothes of someone well off," Ben said, "but you've got the spirit of someone from Fisher's Row. I know you did quite a bit of damage out in Wethrintir. What are you? A simple magus that can sling energy around? Maybe an Elementalist with control over one of the elements? With all of the physical damage to the town you caused it would make sense that you have some control over one of the elements. You certainly didn't destroy a few buildings with just your mouth."

"Maybe I am a magic user. Maybe we both are," she said, nodding towards Nolan. "Do you think the four of you could handle us?"

"Of course we could handle you, even if I believed you were magic users, which I don't. We're professional bounty hunters, miss. We train to take down any mark."

"And how do you fools know we aren't magic users?"

Nolan inwardly groaned. Did she have to keep insulting the men?

"Simple," Ben replied, not showing a hint of anger at the insult. "You were about to be taken by a bunch of worthless thieves. A quick show of any kind of magical skill would have scared them off in a--"

Thumping sounds, like the beating of drums, cut him off. All four bounty hunters began looking around for the source of the noise as it grew nearer. Nolan didn't have to guess. He glanced over at Ezzy.

She was actually smirking at the men!

"Well," she said in a sarcastic tone, "Let's see if you are trained for this."

A slight tremor in the stone bridge made them all glance to the east. Paz's head wobbled into view first as the Vilathos stomped its way up the bridge. By the time its massive iron body was completely in view, the bounty hunters had managed to overcome their shock.

"Vilathos!" one of the men yelled.

"Take out the one controlling it!" Ben yelled.

He was pointing at Nolan.

"Dung," Nolan murmured and immediately threw himself to the ground. There was a whooshing sound as something flew over his head. The move saved him from being struck by whatever the men had thrown, but he landed hard on his bad knee. A sharp pain jolted up his leg, making his stomach churn. He would be feeling that for days to come. Assuming they survived tonight, of course.

Rolling to the side, he watched as Paz crashed into the group of bounty hunters. Bodies dove in every direction. Three of the men, including Ben, had managed to jump out of the way, but the fourth man had not been quick enough. The force of Paz charging knocked the man clear into the air and over the side of the bridge. The remaining bounty hunters were back on their feet in a heartbeat, but by that time, Ezzy was in full control of the situation.

She had Paz grab one of the men with a giant hand and lift him off the ground. Another of the men pulled a dagger from his belt, but let out a yelp as Paz tossed his friend right at him. The two crashed together and rolled about in a mess of bodies. Ben tried to get to Nolan, but had to dodge out of the way as Paz took a swipe at him.

Unfortunately that did not stop the bounty hunter from releasing a small knife in Nolan's direction.

The blade struck the front of Nolan's left shoulder and sunk in deep. While not a heavy blade, the force of the impact did knock him from his side to his back. The pain was intense, but he was used to worse. It was nothing compared to the process of bonding a Vilathos.

Thankfully, by the time Nolan managed to roll back to his side, the fight was over. The two unnamed bounty hunters were fleeing back towards the west side of the river, and Ben was in the firm grasp of Paz. Four metal fingers were wrapped around the man's torso, leaving his arms and hands free. Ben was struggling against the massive metal hand, but had a defeated look on his face.

"If you are going to kill me," he said, looking directly at Nolan, "get it over with."

Letting out a laugh, Ezzy approached the dangling man.

"Speak to me. Paz is under my control. I won't kill you, but I am disappointed in all of the trouble you've caused. I had hoped to get more time with my family before leaving the city. Hearing you were after me ruined my night."

Nolan let out a loud cough.

Ezzy gave him an apologetic look.

"Of course that also includes the knife sticking out of your shoulder. I thought that went without saying." She turned back to Ben while pointing a thumb in Nolan's direction. "I'm going to have to get a Healer or Saniteal to look at his wound now. And that will cost money."

Ben smirked at her...until she began going through his pockets.

"Oh you can't be serious," Ben growled down at her. "You're robbing me?"

"Not robbing. You are just paying for my friend's medical bill."

"If you think for one second I'll give you a single co--"

Ben was cut off as Paz began to violently shake him in the air.

"Sorry," Ezzy cupped a hand to her ear, "what was that? I didn't quite hear what you said."

Paz gave the man a few more shakes before it stopped.

"Fine, fine." Reaching into the back of his pants, Ben pulled out a small pouch and started working at the drawstrings holding it closed.

"I'm sure whatever you have will be more than enough."

Ezzy snatched the pouch out of his hands. He tried to grab it from her, but Paz lifted him higher into the air.

"Now wait just a minute, if you think I'm going to let you just walk off with all of my money, you're mistaken."

"Oh, I know you weren't going to just let us walk off either way. That's why I got your coins first."

"Wha--"

Whatever else Ben was going to say, it changed to a surprised yell as Paz threw the man over the side of the bridge.

"Ezzy!" Nolan yelled as he struggled to his feet. It was difficult to do with a throbbing knee and favoring his left shoulder. "What did you do?"

"I made sure he didn't follow us, that's what I did. The river will hopefully take him out of the city before he can make it to shore. I doubt he will come right after us, soaking wet and tired from swimming against the current."

"He might since you robbed him of all of his money."

"Oh, I doubt it's all of his money. No one is stupid enough to travel with all of their money on them. Plus, I don't know how you could feel bad for the man with his knife still sticking out of your shoulder."

He decided not to argue with that.

"Yes well, pull this thing out of me and let's get going. I'll wrap it as we walk. We'll have to wait until we get to Shade to find someone to patch this up. Let's get off this bridge before anyone else shows up."

"Oh, I can patch you up. We can't leave that wound unattended for the thirteen or so days it will take to walk to Shade. It could get infected or something."

"We can't go looking for a Healer now. It's too late. Plus, that's the first place Ben will look."

"Yes, I realize that obviously. Once he is out of the river, he'll probably have the other fellow that went for a swim round up their men so they can watch the eastern gate and road tonight. They won't expect us to just hole up for the night. I say we stay at the Lost Souls Inn on the east side of the river and then head east out of the city early in the morning. We can travel all the way to the Unyielding Wall and then follow it south to Shade, avoiding the road altogether."

"That might actually be a good idea." Or a horrible one, but with his injury, the thought of traveling without even getting it stitched up made him agree with her

"Don't act so surprised. I can come up with good ideas when given the chance."

"Yes, except nowhere in your plan did you describe how I'm going to fix up my shoulder."

"Oh, that part's easy."

Walking over, she grinned at him. In a flash, she grabbed the handle of the knife and yanked it out of his shoulder. Nolan couldn't help the yelp of pain that escaped his mouth. The knife hurt more coming out than it did going in. And the girl could have been gentler about it. Placing a hand over the wound, he put as much pressure on it as he could.

"Great," he grunted, "now it's out. But what about the wound that you made worse with your oh-so-gentle hands?"

"Simple. We get a room, I break out my sewing supplies, and I patch you up like I would a pair of pants. And here I thought all of those sewing lessons my mother taught me were a waste of time. Well, I'll have to tell her she was right when we come back to the city. Now let's go before you bleed out all over the bridge.'

Ezzy took his hand and began pulling him along. As they finished crossing the bridge and moved into the less developed east bank of the river, all Nolan could think about were all of Ezzy's badly patched clothes.

Chapter Ten

CUTS AND BREAKS

"See, that wasn't so horrible."

Nolan glared at her, but Ezzy just returned the look with a smile.

"I think I did a good job for my first time working with skin instead of cloth."

He continued to glare. Ezzy's smile waned slightly.

"You might have a bigger scar than what a healer might leave, but it stopped bleeding and it will heal...I think."

That earned her a roll of the eyes before Nolan rose from the bed.

The rooms at the Lost Souls Inn were as plain and unadorned as an empty crypt. A single lantern hung against the back wall opposite the door and did little to light up the room this late at night. Two beds took up one side of the room, two sitting chairs and a small table the other. Other than the lantern, nothing adorned the walls, and the wooden floor was bare. All of the rooms on the upper floors of the inn were arranged the same way. The inn was mainly used by those wanting to visit their deceased relatives in the Endless Tombs, and the barren rooms fit in with the mood of those that used them.

Except Ezzy and Nolan were not visiting the Endless Tombs. At the moment, they were trying to keep from becoming new residents of the temple's dark and maze-like halls.

"I suppose it's acceptable," Nolan replied as he paced about the room. "Some people say that scars are attractive on men."

Ezzy raised an eyebrow. "Oh? I didn't even know you cared about attracting the opposite sex."

"Well, no, I don't care about--"

"I'm just teasing. I don't want to hear about what kind of women you like or anything like that."

"Maybe YOU should try looking for someone to settle down with--"

"That's none of your concern." Ezzy stood up and glared at him as anger flushed her face. Nolan let out a laugh, which of course made her scowl deepen. "We have more important things to worry about right now."

"True, no point in thinking about a social life when you have a bounty on your head."

"Oh, I don't care about that," Ezzy laughed as she waved his comment and her anger away. "I meant getting to Shade. It's going to take us longer to get to Shade if we avoid the road. We're going to need more rations."

"We'll just buy them from the inn."

"Oh. I didn't realize that an inn also provided supplies."

"Yes, Ezzy. Now knowing how bare bones this inn is, I'm sure the rations won't be very appetizing, but they will get us the rest of the way there."

"Good. Then if you are feeling up to it, why don't you go and get our supplies so we can get going."

"Fine."

Grabbing his walking stick, Nolan was half-way out the door when he turned back around.

"Stay here."

Ezzy just smiled and batted her eyelashes at him. That earned her a huff from the man before he left, slamming the door behind him.

Ezzy let out a laugh. It was so easy to mess with him. She knew all of the right topics that would bother him. Of course, he knew the same about her. And he knew the difference between topics that annoyed her to no end and topics that could cut her deeply. He never touched the latter. Just like she never mentioned the toll that bonding Vithalos had on his mind.

He should retire. Even when she was young, the toll of being a Thaljori had started showing on him. The last new bond he had done for Ezzy's father had put him out for almost two dozen days. Even a re-bond was hard on him. With her last re-bond with Paz, Nolan hadn't been able to speak properly for two days. And that had been five or six years ago. Who knows how it would affect him now.

The thought made her nervous, and she focused on her bond. Paz was there on the other end of the connection, sitting exactly where she had sent him. There weren't many places you could hide a Vilathos in the city, especially one like hers, but thankfully there were a few places people seldom went.

Ezzy focused harder and an image started to form in her mind. Through Paz's jewelled eyes, she could see the worn cobble road, the lake to the west, and the huge dilapidated building where Paz hid. She had placed him behind a large vine-covered column with the grass tall enough to almost cover his waist. People feared that place. Said it was haunted. Ezzy didn't believe in such things. Everyone knew a person's soul was released by the Soulbearers and sent to Kaz'ren.

The abandoned temple of Ze'an did give her the creeps though.

She had Paz take a look around, curious to see how the fallen temple looked. She hadn't been there since she was a kid, and it had been a mess back then. The dozen or so years surprisingly hadn't done that much more damage to the building. It even looked like--

The image started to blur for a moment, and Ezzy blinked her eyes reflexively even though they had nothing to do with what she was seeing. Shaking her head with chagrin, she instead focused harder on her connection to Paz. He wasn't that far away. It shouldn't be this hard to see through his--

Oh no.

The realization hit her just as the image blurred and then vanished.

It had been less than two years! NO!

Ezzy grasped at the bond. Clawed at it. Felt it slip through her mental fingers, felt its strength wane.

No, no, no, no, no...

She could do nothing as the bond shrunk to thread thin and then was gone. There was nothing there.

Ezzy braced herself.

The whiplash of the bond dissolving hit her mind stronger than any physical blow she had ever felt. Her body convulsed and she lost all control. She blacked out before she could feel the impact of her crumpling body hit the floor.

***

"Thank you," Nolan said, swinging the pack of rations over his uninjured shoulder. The pack was light enough that it didn't much irritate his bad knee. The inn-keeper's wife just nodded in reply. The owners really were not a friendly bunch. It kept with their reputation though and fit in with their location close to the Endless Tombs.

He made his way back through the common room. Not a single person sat at the tables. As infrequently as he had visited inns and taverns throughout most of his life, he was used to at least some signs of life, regardless of the time of day. Here, it felt like a funeral procession had just left. He moved back through the room as quickly as he could, up the stairs, and into the room he and Ezzy would share for the night.

The bag slid from his shoulder as he saw Ezzy convulsing on the floor. In a few quick and painful steps he was by her side, lifting her head with one hand as he grabbed a pillow from the bed with his other hand and slid it underneath. Her eyes were closed, her breathing ragged, and drool ran out of both corners of her mouth. This was the first time Nolan had actually been present when Ezzy's bond had dissolved. The sight of her in this condition broke his heart.

"Ezzy," he whispered, "Ezzy, I need you to wake up."

Her body stopped twitching but she remained unresponsive.

"Ezzy, I need to know where you hid Paz."

Giving her a shake, he gently pulled one of her eyelids open. Her eye was rolled back. Not good.

"Come on, Ezzy. You're stronger than this." That was a lie, no one was strong enough to just shrug it off when a bond broke. "We need to get you to Paz so I can fix this."

Still nothing. Rising, he looked around the room until he spotted the pitcher of water provided by the inn. Grabbing it off the floor, he stood over her and hesitated for a moment to brace himself for her indignant screams. It couldn't be helped. Their situation was too dangerous at the moment for her to be out of it for a few days and for Paz to be who-knows-where, standing as useless as a statue.

With a sigh only he could hear, he dumped the entire contents of the pitcher onto her face.

As soon as the water hit her, she spluttered and sat up. Her eyes looked around, although they were glazed and unfocused.

"What...I...where am I?"

"Ezzy," he leaned down so she could see him better, "are you alright? You need to tell me--"

She struck him once in the chest and sent another punch directly towards his face. Nolan barely dodged it, if falling backwards in pain could be considered dodging a blow.

"Ezzy, what--"

"Who are you? Where am I? Have I been kidnapped?"

Wonderful.

"Ezzy, it's me, Nolan. I know it's difficult, but you need to try and focus. Collect your thoughts. Remember what is going on."

"Nolan? Are you here to bond me with one of my dolls again?" Her voice had taken on a higher pitch and her gaze was still empty. This was bad.

"Ezzy, I haven't bonded you to a doll in a long time. You're an adult now. You have a Vilathos of your own, and I need to know where you hid it."

"A Vilathos of my own? Father would never let me do that."

"Esmerelda, your father is dead. He abandoned you."

A harsh statement, and mostly untrue, but he didn't have time to spare her feelings. With bounty hunters on their tail, and his injured shoulder, Ezzy's broken link couldn't have come at a worse time. He would shake the girl silly if it came to it.

Thankfully, his words struck home. Her eyes started to water as her lip began to tremble. That only lasted a moment, and then that cold steel that seemed to have taken root since her father's death returned to her eyes. The cold gaze she directed his way seemed to drink up the tears that had started to form. When she finally spoke, it was with a whisper, but the force of her words put a shiver down his spine.

"Get away from me."

"I'm sorry, Ezzy, I needed you to focus."

"You don't know anything about my father or what he did for my family. You only graced us with your presence when you wanted to make some money."

The words hurt more than he expected, mostly from the initial surprise at hearing them. Was that what she actually thought?

No, she thinks more of me than that, and she knows I respected her father a great deal. She is just lashing out.

At least, that's what he hoped. He extended a hand to help her up and pulled it right back with the look she gave him. Well, maybe she would just need a little more time to get her bearings.

"Ezzy, you know I didn't really mean--"

"Not another word. You're lucky I can barely see straight, otherwise I'd make sure you felt worse than I do now. Knife wound or not. Now what do you want?"

"Uh..." Not sure whether to keep quiet like she said or answer her question, Nolan shuffled about in place.

Ezzy rolled her eyes and then immediately brought a hand up to rub at them. After a few moments, she finally spoke.

"Right. Paz. You want to know where Paz is hiding. I put him by the temple to Ze'an. No one ever goes near there, especially at night."

"Good. I'll start getting our things together, and we can go fix your bond. Do you want me to get your things?"

"I can handle that myself, thank you very much." Ezzy tried to rise but immediately fell forward. She was barely able to keep her face from smacking into the ground. "Alright. You can get my things ready as well. I'm going to examine this section of the floor boards."

"Of course. Of course. Right away."

He busied himself with gathering their things. They had kept most of their possessions packed in case they had to make a quick exit, but there were still a few odds and ends that needed to be put away or better organized. As Nolan moved about the room, he constantly checked on Ezzy. The most she did while he moved about was roll onto her back and stare at the ceiling. Her eyes did seem clearer though. The bigger the Vilathos, the more painful a severed bond, but Ezzy's resilience was amazing. She truly was a strong woman.

"All set."

He dropped the last of their packs by the door and turned to find Ezzy climbing one of the beds. He took a step forward to help then stopped as she shot him another look. Instead, he stood there and watched as she clawed her way back to her feet. She stood there looking stronger than he expected, although she did keep a hand on the bed. Again, Nolan couldn't help but be amazed and feel a little proud of her.

"Alright," she grunted, giving him a withering stare, "you can help me now."

Nolan raised an eyebrow, which of course was the wrong thing to do.

"I'm not a fool, Nolan." Her voice could have frozen the lake. "Despite the fact that you are an insensitive moron, I'm not so full of pride that I would think I could make it out of here on my own. My legs feel about as stable as a wet noodle, all I can see of you is an annoying blur, and I'm alternating between feeling like I'm going to get sick or pass out. I know I need your help."

"Good, because I can't imagine how--"

"Helping me to walk does not involve talking to me right now."

"Understood."

Nolan grabbed two of the lighter bags and gently strapped it to Ezzy's shoulders. Then, after grabbing the last remaining pack and his walking stick, he hooked his arm around her and got them moving. It was awkward at first, between his limp, his staff, and the packs moving around on their backs, but it became much smoother by the time they made it to the stairs. When they were out the front door and into the cold night air, he had things under control.

This close to morning and at this time of year, the streets were empty. Behind the inn, the temple to Kaz'ren peaked over the roof while the Endless Tombs towered over everything else. Nolan took a moment to catch his breath and adjust the packs before he got them moving up the street. The temple to Ze'an was north of them on the southeast side of the lake, at the end of this road. Fields of untended grass sat between the last buildings of the city and the temple. After all, who would be foolish enough to build anywhere near the temple of the god of the Abyss?

They walked uninterrupted all the way to the temple, stopping once they reached its massive doors. The temple was a combination of decades of neglect, vandalism from the more fervent worshippers of Alistar, and youths trying to prove their bravery, which turned the building into a dilapidated mess. Stone columns lay where they had toppled, stained glass windows were smashed beyond recognition, and even the thick wooden doors were splintered and dangling off their hinges. Add to that the light of all three moons making shadows dance about this late at night, and a person couldn't help but be put off by the place.

"Over there," Ezzy pointed off to the right side of the building. "Paz is behind those columns."

With a nod, Nolan helped her over to the Vithalos. Sure enough, the hulking metal form was standing where she had directed it. Thankfully, when their connection had broken, the Vilathos hadn't toppled over. Nolan had heard it fall against stone once before and had no doubt that the commotion would have drawn people even this late at night.

Leaning Ezzy up against the wall, Nolan placed one hand on her shoulder and another on the leg of the Vilathos. There was no time to waste, and no point in preparing either of them for what came next. Best to get to it. He cleared his mind and focused his energy.

Everything else fell away into darkness. Ezzy and the Vilathos became vague outlines of energy, a golden color that swirled about them both. From where their heads would be, a wisp of energy fluttered like a flag about to detach from its pole. That was the connection. That was what he needed to fix.

Unlike an initial bonding, where the energy of the person resisted becoming part of the Vilathos, fixing a bond was much easier in comparison. Those two connections wanted to be back together. Neither was whole without the other. To the lifeless Vilathos, not being connected had no effect, but to Ezzy it was like losing a part of her very spirit. That was what caused her body to weaken and befuddled her mind.

Focus. Even a reconnection can have problems. This is not the time for introspection.

Gathering his will, Nolan "reached out" with his mind and grasped both cords. They writhed about in his grip, the energy having a life of its own and not understanding what was going on. It fought his mental grasp, but decades of experience won out. Slowly but surely, Nolan began to pull the two edges towards each other. The closer they became, the less the energies fought him. When they touched, they melded into each other like two old friends embracing after years of being apart.

Now for the difficult part...

Unchecked, the energies could flow entirely back into Ezzy or into the Vilathos. If they flowed into Ezzy, she would lose all connection with the Vilathos. Even worse, the energy from the Vilathos had changed. Even though it came close to matching Ezzy's energy, it would never be the same again. If it all flowed back into her, she would have two different energies vying for control, never able to become one. The stress of wild energy raging inside of Ezzy would destroy her. In less than a year, the girl's mind would be reduced to mush.

If the energies all flowed into the Vilathos...well, that would leave nothing left for Ezzy.

Grasping the energies as tightly as he could, Nolan fought to control the flow. He felt nothing else, his entire attention gauging the tide of the two energies, adjusting his grip so that the weaker flow had more freedom while he limited the stronger one. It went back and forth, Ezzy's energy trying to rush into Paz, then instantly flipping to Paz's energy almost overwhelming Ezzy. Each time the flow changed directions, the surge grew a little weaker.

Finally, after what may have been minutes or hours, Nolan felt the two energies even out. He held them a few moments longer, making sure there wouldn't be one last surge. A surge that could destroy a person's mind instantaneously. It was all a part of the risk, and he had gotten used to it happening with strangers. But Ezzy was no stranger and he would never risk her life. When he was content that the connection was solid, he let go. The world came rushing back, overwhelming his senses and hammering him to his knees.

"Are you...better...?" he panted. Each breath burned in his chest while their sound tore at his ears.

"Yes, I have control of him again. Are you going to be ok?"

The concern in her voice would have been comforting to hear if the sound didn't make his head feel like exploding. His vision swam, the dark green of the grass beneath him swirled about and made his eyes burn. A cold breeze touched his skin, but it felt like razor blades raking across his face. The musky smell of the old temple mixed in with the smell of being outside, overloaded his senses and made him nauseous.

He welcomed the grey clouds crowding out his vision--a telltale sign that his mind was about to shut down. It was a relief when the blessed blackness covered his senses, and he sank into unconsciousness.

Chapter Eleven

ON THE MOVE

Nolan opened his eyes to the three moons hanging high above him in a sea of stars. The green moon sparkled like an emerald in the sky. The blue and red moons seemed just as bright, although they were higher in the sky and not as grand. The vast array of stars dotting the sky looked like tiny flames straining against the emptiness above him. Used to a life in the city where the buildings and lights diminished the effect of the stars, being out in the open made him feel like the tiniest speck in a much bigger universe.

He licked dry lips with an even drier tongue and tried to sit up. That's when he realized he couldn't move. Panic set in as memories of previous events flooded back in. Had they been caught? How long had he been out? He struggled against his bonds, which only made his knee and shoulder ache. He let out little grunts as he discovered his weakened body couldn't budge against the restraints.

"Calm down." Ezzy's voice, containing an uncharacteristic amount of concern, came from his right. Turning his head, he found the woman holding a stick with some kind of skewered animal over a fire. A small cooking pot had also been set up over the flames. "You're just wrapped up in blankets. You've been out a while, and I wrapped you up in a blanket cocoon to keep you from freezing."

"How long?"

"Five days."

Five days. From a simple re-bonding. He was getting much worse. Glancing down at his prison of blankets, it only took Nolan a moment to figure out how to get himself out. It took considerably longer than he would have liked to shed the blankets in his weakened condition. The cold air of the season immediately bit him and he moved closer to the fire to fend it off.

"When you are feeling up to it, you should try to eat something. I've gotten you to take water and broth in your stupor, but nothing else. I have a vegetable stew cooking in the pot, I can dish you a bowl."

"Thank you, yes, I think that would help." Looking down, he realized he was in a different set of clothes. "Did you change my clothes?"

Her face went red, and she turned her attention back to the fire.

"Yes. You had...err..."

"It's ok, please, for both our sakes, don't say it."

An after-effect of the process was complete loss of control over his body. Including his bodily functions.

"Thank you," Ezzy said, the relief clear in her voice. "I just tossed the clothes away. I hope you don't mind."

Nolan wasn't exactly happy with the waste of clothes, but he couldn't handle continuing a conversation about his lack of bladder control.

"I understand."

She handed him a bowl of stew and then fell silent. Very few people had seen him in that state, and Ezzy had never been there for more than the first few moments after the effects knocked Nolan unconscious. Her father had done an excellent job of protecting Ezzy from seeing that side of the bonding process. But he was gone now. It was a foolish desire, but Nolan had always hoped she would never have to see him like that.

"I'm sorry."

Nolan could only stare at Ezzy. She had actually apologized? Was he still unconscious and dreaming?

"I know I was harsh in Lurthalan," she continued, "but you know how angry I get when anything negative is said about my father. I've come to realize that you only said those things to get me going. Father considered you a friend, not just another hireling, and I think of you as...well... like an uncle."

Shaking off the initial shock, he did his best to put on a smile. "And how long did it take you to realize this?"

She returned his smile and let out a short laugh. "Only two or three days into the trip. Certainly after I had to change you like a baby."

<hr />

He could feel his cheeks heating, but at least Ezzy hadn't laced her words with scorn. If she was trying to make a joke of it, then she was probably trying to help him not feel so awkward about it. It was her method of making peace, and although it wasn't how most civilized people would apologize, Nolan appreciated the gesture.

"Well, I've known you since you were a baby and making a mess in your clothes, so I guess we've come full circle. Enough about that though. Where are we?'

"Look for yourself." She gestured to her left.

Towering above them less than a day's journey away to the east was the Unyielding Wall. The wall was a marvel of construction, reaching high into the sky almost as far as the Skyfall Mountains to the west. No one knew who had constructed it or why. Historians thought that at one time all of the races knew where it had come from, but so much had been lost during the Plague that it could be anyone's guess now. All people knew was that the most powerful magic could only dent the massive stone blocks. It was also said that being in close proximity to the wall for too long could do strange things to a person, but that was just hearsay. After all, the village of Shade had been built in its shadow a long time ago, and the people there seemed normal.

For the most part at least.

"That doesn't exactly tell me where we are. The wall is said to stretch from coast to coast, although the only people that would know for sure are those infected by the Plague in the north and the Shadaer Umdaer in the south. That's a lot of land to cover."

"I don't know," she said with a roll of her eyes. "Somewhere north of Shade and southwest of Lurthalan. It's not like anyone other than those fools down in Shade settle anywhere close to that monstrosity. It took a whole day to get this close to the wall, and we've been traveling south for four more days since then. So, where does that put us?"

"Another six or seven days of travel left until we get to Shade, I would guess. I don't exactly know how fast you and Paz have been moving."

"Neither do I. Not a whole lot this close to the wall to use as a landmark. We did pass the last farm this afternoon."

"That helps. We should only be about a day from the forest, and then it will probably take us another four to make our way through the trees since we won't have a clear path to travel."

"Excellent." Ezzy handed over the stick she had been holding over the fire. "Have some meat. I caught it myself."

His eyebrows raised in surprise as he took the stick from her.

"What? I can take care of myself, and I figured if I caught some food, it would save some of the supplies we bought in case we have trouble catching a meal later."

He bit into the meat. The meat was moist, and even had the flavor of a few spices to it.

They hadn't packed any spices.

"This tastes surprisingly good," he said in-between bites. "I didn't know you knew how to cook...what is this again?"

"Rabbit, I think."

"You think?"

"I mean, yes, rabbit. Just eat it already if your stomach can handle more. We should get some sleep so we can get an early start tomorrow."

Nolan let out a laugh and did as he was told. No point on calling her out for a rabbit she had clearly gotten from a trader or hunter. That must have been an interesting conversation, with him unconscious and tied to Paz's back. He hoped she had been smart enough to say very little about their situation.

Finishing up the rabbit, Nolan went to stand, but his legs refused to cooperate.

"Just sit and rest. It would be good if you had enough energy to walk tomorrow. I'll clean up."

"Thank you."

Crawling back over to his blankets, he wrapped himself up as tightly as he could. From his spot on the ground, he watched Ezzy move about the camp. She really was quite the capable girl. Ezzy could probably handle this whole quest for justice by herself if she wanted. If only she could control her temper. For the most part, she was a very well put-together woman with a good head on her shoulders. Nolan had seen others in her situation growing up in a powerful and rich family become spoiled elitists that treated everyone as a servant. Both the boys and the girls. But not Ezzy.

"Gutter piss." she shouted, dropping the pot and dumping its contents all over the ground. "That's hot!"

No, certainly not an overly-refined and stuffy lady. Nolan let himself chuckle until she shot him a glare. He quickly rolled over onto his side, letting her gaze dig into his back so she couldn't see his grin. Instead he contented himself with thinking about the journey ahead.

One day to the forest, and then four to Shade. That, of course, was being generous. Once they reached the forest, without traveling on the road they would be forced to navigate the dense population of trees. That would slow them down considerably. Add in the fact that neither of them were expert outdoorsmen. If they weren't careful, they could get themselves turned around and waste time traveling in the wrong direction. They could handle losing a day or two, but anything more than that and they would run out of supplies. Then they would be forced to find the road that stretched from Lurthalan to Shade through the woods and hope they ran into someone with food to trade and not another group of bounty hunters.

Or worse, the group that Ezzy and Paz had beaten and robbed. They certainly would be looking for revenge now just as much as the bounty.

"Nolan!"

Throwing off his covers, Nolan sat up and hurriedly looked around. Were they under attack? When he didn't see any immediate threat, he shot a questioning glance at Ezzy.

"I put that bowl of broth next to you a while ago. It's probably cold by now. Have you just been lying there the whole time? I wasn't paying attention while I set up our tents."

"Oh...yes, I guess my mind wandered..."

"It's ok." She gave him a pitying look. He hated that. Hated that she knew his mind was starting to go. "Why don't you eat a little of the broth and head to bed. You need more rest."

"Of course."

"Don't pout," she ordered in her normal, commanding tone. "Eat and go to bed. That's an order."

Most people would have found that tone abrasive, but Nolan appreciated it. Ezzy knew what was happening to his mind, but more importantly she knew better than to dwell on it for too long. Acting normal was the best way she could help them both not think about his condition.

"I don't see you eating!"

"Ok, ok!"

Ezzy was certainly a spitfire. He downed his meal and got into his tent as fast as he could. As he lay down, his stomach full and his eyes heavy, Nolan's last thought was of how proud Ezzy's father would be of her if he was still alive.

Chapter Twelve

MORE COMPLICATIONS

Temple Bounty - 35 Silver (Alive)

A nudge in Ezzy's back stirred her from her dreams. Dreams of warm beds, fancy clothes, and five-course meals.

"Let me sleep a little longer," Ezzy mumbled. She rolled off her side and onto her stomach, burying her head underneath her arms. "It can't be morning already."

"Get up," an unfamiliar voice growled. "Now."

The words were followed by a harder blow to her side. Not enough to hurt, but it made its point.

Ezzy made a show of slowing turning onto her back. Keeping her eyes closed, she focused on her bond and looked through Paz's eyes. Or at least she tried to look through its eyes. Something was covering them. Not good.

Pushing herself up on her elbows, she opened her eyes to find she had been pulled out of her tent. More disturbing was the point of an arrow was almost touching her nose.

"Don't try anything, girl," a female voice said. "I know that metal monstrosity is yours to command. If I so much as hear a squeak from it, this arrow will be the last thing you see."

Ezzy's gaze followed the arrow up, past the tautly drawn bow, to the person wielding it. The woman behind the bow was like no one she had ever seen before. She looked human, with a thin face, her short black hair tied in a knot behind her head. Her dark grey eyes were staring down the shaft of that arrow with a look that showed she meant business. But that was where her similarities to Ezzy's race stopped.

The woman's skin was a crimson red, as if on fire. It was the strangest thing, and she had seen Taruun before with their marble-like skin. The woman's lower canine teeth peeked out from her lips, just enough for Ezzy to see their sharp points. Those grey eyes were slightly slanted and set deeper into her face behind a small nose. Her face might be considered pretty, if on the masculine side, by some if it wasn't for the skin and teeth. She was taller than any woman Ezzy had ever seen before. Taller than most men she knew, and her outfit did little to hide the muscles underneath. If it wasn't for the hint of features only found on a woman, Ezzy might have mistaken her for a man.

She wore the clothes of a bounty hunter. A brown leather shirt adorned with pockets, both large and small, covered her broad shoulders. Leather shorts fell down to her knees while her boots came up almost as high. A thick belt wrapped around her waist, various pouches and knives hung from every open space. The fletching of arrows peeked over her back, as well as the hilt of a weapon.

All in all, the woman was intimidating, and that was saying a lot as Ezzy was rarely intimidated by people.

"Get to your feet. Slowly. Wake your partner. I want to be on the road heading to Lurthalan before the end of the day."

Not feeling the need to respond, Ezzy got to her feet. She couldn't help but stare at the woman. What made her skin that color? Was it paint? The only race Ezzy knew of that had such colorful skin were the Umdaer in the south, but they were supposed to look far from human. Was this woman a mix? Could the races mix?

"Stop staring and move." Her voice made it clear she did not appreciate Ezzy's gaze.

Ezzy gave a smirk then turned her back on the strange woman and moved towards Nolan's still sleeping form. The woman might look tough, but Ezzy wasn't about to show her any fear. The bounty hunter had the advantage, but that could change in an instant. Plus, the bounty was for Ezzy alive, so the woman couldn't kill her. All she needed was one opportunity to catch her off guard.

Kneeling down, she reached into Nolan's tent and shook his foot until the man showed signs of waking.

"Wake up," she said loudly and in an overly sweet voice. "We have company."

"What?" he mumbled. "A merchant or something?"

"No, a particularly ugly bounty hunter."

Ezzy glanced back to see if her words had gotten a rise out of the woman. The bounty hunter smiled at her, showing even more of those two lower fangs. No matter. She was probably used to people calling her names.

"A what?" Nolan pushed the blankets off and sat up. As soon as his eyes found the woman, they widened. "What in the Abyss is that?"

"My name is Shayua Durluin, and I'm the person that will be collecting your bounty," she grunted at him. "Now get up and get your things ready to move."

Shayua lowered her bow as they started to move about the camp, but she kept an arrow nocked. Ezzy put the tents away and gathered their things as Nolan stretched. To Ezzy, he still looked weak. Whatever toll the re-bonding had on his body and mind, it clearly took a while to recover. He looked like he could topple over at any moment.

Once she had things packed, she took a step towards his walking stick. If Shayua wasn't going to let Paz anywhere near them, he at least needed the staff to move on his own.

A sharp twang was the only warning she had before an arrow buried itself right in front of her feet.

She hopped back unable to stop the small shriek from escaping her mouth.

"Do not even think about it," Shayua said. Another arrow was already notched.

"He needs it. He can barely stand as it is, walking without it will be impossible."

"Then let him pick it up. You can carry all of your supplies."

"My Vilathos can--"

"Stay far behind us. I don't want that thing within sprinting distance. You can carry the supplies. The added weight will keep you from trying anything foolish."

"If you say so."

Ezzy grabbed the two packs containing their things and stood glaring at the woman while Nolan limped over and picked up his staff. When everyone was set, Shayua motioned for them to start walking ahead of her. Ezzy watched from the corner of her eye as the woman walked over and pulled her arrow from the ground, returning it to the quiver on her back. Counting the one still ready to fire, the bounty hunter had fifteen or so arrows. Might come in handy to remember that.

Or it might not. Ezzy was just looking for anything she might use to get the upper hand at some point.

They moved in the opposite direction of the Unyielding Wall, Ezzy at the lead with Nolan close behind. Shayua kept her distance behind them, with the bow still ready to fire. They moved at a slow pace. Despite being in excellent shape, two packs were still a lot for Ezzy to lug around. She kept glancing back and each time the other woman's eyes were locked on her. This Shayua was all business. Escape would be a little more difficult than Ezzy had hoped.

"So," she said, glancing back at the towering woman. "Been a bounty hunter long?"

"You don't need to open your mouth to walk."

"That might not be entirely true," Nolan said under his breath.

Why did the man choose now to make jokes? Ezzy shot him a look but decided against commenting on what he said and instead offered, "I'm sure a little conversation won't magically help us escape. It might help the walk go a little faster."

Ezzy received a grunt for a reply. She took that as an opportunity to continue.

"I've never seen anyone that looks...like you. If you were part Taruun that would explain the height, but I've never seen anyone with your skin color before."

"Then I suppose you've never been very far south." Ezzy barely heard the words Shayua muttered. South? From Shade? The Wall was said to do strange things to people, but she had never heard of anything as dramatic as a drastic change in skin color. Certainly she didn't mean Rensen. Where else was there? She had heard of a new village that had been founded a few years ago on the southern end of Rensen forest. Did she mean there? If she meant further south, that would affirm that she had at least a little Umdaer in her.

"So where are you from?"

"Lurthalan."

"No, seriously."

"I was raised in Lurthalan, grew up in the temple of Avien'zia, and made my first kill when I was eleven. That's all you need to know."

"That doesn't explain your...uh, bizarre skin tone."

The woman was next to her in a heartbeat, and just as fast had a hand around Ezzy's throat and lifting her into the air. Ezzy's eyes bulged as she struggled to breathe. She beat at the woman's arms with her hands, but she might as well have been striking hardwood. Even the kicks she sent at the woman's stomach seemed to go unnoticed. And all the while she held Ezzy and her packs in the air.

"Stop it!" Nolan sounded scared, but things were becoming hazy to Ezzy. "You're killing her."

"Listen, little girl." Shayua's voice was low, but she could have been yelling for all Ezzy's oxygen-deprived brain could tell. "You will not mention my skin, or where I come from, or anything about my past. You are a bounty. Nothing more. Do I make myself clear?"

Ezzy tried to say yes, but it came out as a gurgle. She began to nod her head enthusiastically. Anything to be free of the woman's iron grip. Just as spots began to swim across her eyes, Shayua released her. Ezzy crumpled to the ground. The packs slid off her shoulders as she drew in deep, gasping breaths. A hand touched her shoulder, and she flinched but then relaxed as she realized it was Nolan.

"Are you alright?" The amount of concern painted across his face made the pain in her throat soften. A little.

"Yes."

"I don't think you should push her buttons anymore. She seems like the type to forget about money if she gets angry enough."

"I wasn't trying to set her off. I was just curious."

"Well, wherever she's from, they don't seem to like curious people."

"Agreed."

Ezzy let him help her up. Her first instinct was to glare at the other woman, but common sense won out and she instead turned her back to Shayua. Nolan was right, best to just avoid provoking the bounty hunter until they could figure out a way to escape. Speaking of which...

"Can I start my Vithalos moving yet?"

"Yes. But keep it far behind us."

The groan of a bowstring being stretched back was all the warning Ezzy needed to know what would happen if Paz got too close.

They walked on in silence for the rest of the day. In the beginning, Ezzy would glance back from time to time to check on their captor. The only change she noticed in the bounty hunter's demeanor was a deepening scowl that sunk each time their eyes met. It was doubtful they would be able to escape in the middle of the day anyway. Best to wait until night.

By the time they reached the cobblestone road that ran north towards Lurthalan and south towards Shade, the sun was just touching the tips of the Skyfall Mountains to the west. Shayua had them stop and set up camp a little ways off the road. As Ezzy and Nolan made a camp fire and spread out their sleeping bags, Shayua sat and watched them. She had slung her bow over her back, replacing it with a knife she twirled between her crimson fingers. The fact that the woman watched while Ezzy worked started to annoy her to no end. When Shayua told them not to bother with the tents, her annoyance bubbled over.

"I wonder," Ezzy said, not directing the words towards anyone in particular, "if she slipped and cut herself, would she even notice?"

"Ezzy..." Nolan warned.

"It was just a stray thought, Nolan. I mean, if she bled could we even tell? Or is her blood a different color than ours?"

"Shall we compare?"

Shayua rose and started walking towards her, knife in hand. Ezzy tried to take a step back but the stronger woman grabbed her wrist. She yanked and strained, trying to get her arm free, until Shayua brought the knife right up to Ezzy's face.

"I bleed red." Shayua slid the blade across the back of her own hand, twisting it to show Ezzy while keeping an iron grip on her wrist. "Let's see if it's the same shade as yours."

"Stop this!" Nolan took a few steps forward but stopped as Shayua pointed the blade in his direction.

"I am simply answering her question. The spoiled girl needs to learn that she cannot always say whatever she wishes."

"Yes, I agree. It's a lesson I've been trying to teach her this past year. She is a difficult student."

"Maybe that is because you coddle her. I will not be that gentle."

Ezzy gave a squeak as the woman placed the edge of the blade against the back of her hand.

"Stop," Nolan pleaded. "Don't hurt her."

Shayua glanced back at him over her shoulder for a few moments, then grunted and released Ezzy's hand.

"Think of this as her last chance to watch her words. The bounty just says to bring her in alive, it says nothing about what condition she must be in."

"I understand. She will watch her tongue. You have my word on it."

He glared at Ezzy. She returned his look for a moment, then rolled her eyes and nodded. Shayua missed the gesture as her attention was focused on Nolan.

"Good." Shayua licked the blood off her hand. "I will hold you responsible for reminding her of what will happen if she steps out of line. To both of you."

"Understood."

"Get to work on our dinner. I expect you both to turn in as soon as we eat and the sun sets. We will be leaving as soon as the sun climbs over the wall."

"I don't think that's going to happen," Ezzy said. Shayua took a threatening step towards her, but Ezzy stopped her with one raised hand and pointed up the road with the other. "We have visitors."

Seven men were walking down the road. Each had a hand on a weapon.

"You two stay seated." Shayua already had her bow back in her hands and an arrow nocked. "I want them to come to us. Don't say a word."

The men were close enough now that Ezzy could make out their faces.

"I don't think talking is going to help."

The man leading the rest was the bounty hunter, Ben.

Chapter Thirteen

FIGHTING OVER A PRIZE

"You're not going to be able to talk to them." Between the red-skinned bounty hunter and the ones she had beaten up and robbed, it was easy for Ezzy to decide whom she would rather have as a captor. "Those men are bounty hunters as well. We've run into them before."

"Then it won't be a problem," Shayua replied. Her bow remained drawn.

"You don't understand. The last time I saw the man leading them, I had my Vithalos toss him into the Melcoi River."

"After robbing him," Nolan chimed in.

"Well, he was rude."

"It doesn't matter what you did," Shayua barked. "If they are bounty hunters, they will follow the code. I'm the one that caught you, so your bounty is mine."

"I don't think this man cares about rules or codes or whatever you bounty hunters follow."

"You know nothing. The rules were set by the goddess Avien'zia herself. A true bounty hunter will not break them."

"If you say so. Then why do you still have an arrow aimed in their direction?"

"Just be quiet."

Ezzy did as she was told. It was difficult to just sit there with Ben's eyes locked on her as his group approached. He did not look happy. None of the men looked happy. Had any of the others been there that night? She hadn't paid them much attention.

"That's close enough," Shayua called out when the men were a stone's throw away. "What are your intentions?"

The group stopped. Most had a hand on their weapons, but none had drawn a blade. Except Ben. He had a knife in his hand as he took a few more steps forward. When he spoke, his voice was calm but firm.

"My name is Ben Karren. Those two sitting at your camp are my bounties. I plan on taking them back to Lurthalan."

"Unfortunately I have claimed them already."

Ben's eyes narrowed.

"I had already claimed them days ago. They--"

"You cannot claim them if you cannot hold on to them."

"This one had her Vithalos beat up my men. Then she robbed me and tossed me into the river. I'm not about to let--"

"None of this matters. By Avien'zia's Code, they are mine."

Ben's jaw dropped. His men shuffled about nervously behind him. Despite the situation she currently found herself in, Ezzy felt a smile creep its way onto her face. She had to admit she was starting to like Shayua's straight-forwardness. As long as it wasn't directed at her, of course.

"Now," Shayua continued, "if you wish, I can return whatever money they have on them to you.

"No, that's not good enough," Ben spluttered, finally able to find words. "I've suffered too many insults and put too much work into hunting these two down to let them go now."

"The Code states--"

"Damn the Code! They are mine, and I plan on teaching the girl some humility on the way back to Lurthalan."

"Watch what you say when it comes to the Code. You tread on dangerous ground." Shayua's voice had grown cold and her bow had come up slightly.

"No one follows the Code. Now stand aside before I decide--urk!"

To say Ben looked surprised as the arrow thudded into his right thigh would be an understatement. The impact was enough to stagger him backwards and twist him around, but to the man's credit he was able to stay on his feet. He gripped the arrow shaft with both hands and stared at it. His mouth worked but nothing came out. Shayua, on the other hand, already had another arrow ready to fly. Its point rapidly shifting directions to aim at each of the remaining six men in turn. Her eyes were narrowed, and her grimace let both of her lower incisors peek out of her lips.

"The Code is everything." A fire touched Shayua's voice. "Without the Code, we are nothing more than thugs and murderers. If you are either of those things, I will grind you all beneath my boots."

"You can't take us all." Ben replied through clenched teeth.

Ezzy marveled at the man's confidence. Even with an arrow in his leg, he still made demands. Despite the way the arrow was causing him to lean to one side, Ben raised his knife and seemed ready to fight.

"I can kill enough of you with my bow before you get close enough to have a fair chance against the rest in hand-to-hand combat. Are your men ready to risk their lives when a single arrow could kill them before they take a few steps?"

"You have no idea who you're dealing with. Men! Show her our colors."

Each man with Ben in turn pulled out an orange piece of cloth from their various pockets and bags and raised them to their heads. Seven men now stood before them with orange headbands.

"By the Abyss..." Nolan groaned.

"Should those pieces of cloth mean something to me?" Shayua looked at each man in turn. "Are the headbands magic of some kind?"

"Not magic," Ben grunted. "But they do bind us as brothers. You might not have heard of the Orange Hound gang in Lurthalan. But you will when we take your beaten body back there. We're going to make sure everyone knows our name. Just like they will know that one bounty hunter tried to stand against us and was put down like a fire-faced half-breed deserves."

The words were barely out of the man's mouth when he launched himself to the side, one of Shayua's arrows passing through the space where his head had been. With a shout, the rest of Ben's men charged. Two never made it more than a few steps as an arrow pierced their chest and a third was knocked off his feet as one of Shayua's arrows struck his shoulder. Then, the world became chaos.

Shayua tangled one man's weapon up in her bowstring and threw him to the ground as he charged in, which disarmed them both. She twisted to avoid the thrust of a blade and caught a second man with a right cross that freed a few of his teeth. He hit the ground and remained in a crumpled heap. Then the other men overwhelmed her.

The last uninjured man discarded his weapon and tried to tackle Shayua. While she was trying to throw him off, Ben and the man who had been struck in the shoulder joined the fight, diving at her feet. Shayua was able to stay up for a moment, but when the one she had initially tossed joined the fight, she was strong-armed to the ground. Bodies flailed about as the four men wrestled to pin Shayua's arms and legs. She was strong, but the men had numbers as well as weight on their side and were quickly getting the upper hand.

The thought of escape flashed through Ezzy's mind, but only for a moment. There was flatland all around them and even though she might be able to get away, there was no way that Nolan could move very fast. Plus, something about seeing the woman at the mercy of those men didn't sit right with her.

"We should help!" Ezzy shouted, charging towards the melee.

"What? Wait!" Nolan's words were lost to her as she dove at the closest man.

She collided with the uninjured man, her momentum carrying him off of Shayua. The man smelled of tobacco and sweat. They rolled around on the grass, trying to jockey for position. The man ended up on top of her, both of his hands going for her neck. While his hands went to choke, hers struck instead, punching him directly in the throat. A sickening gurgle escaped his mouth as both of his hands left her neck and grasped at his own. With a twist of her hips she dislodged the man from on top of her. He fell onto his side and continued to struggle to take in his breath. Not wasting any time, Ezzy rose and planted a quick kick to the man's face.

His gurgling and thrashing stopped. Ezzy spun to find her next target.

Shayua stood over two of the men, their bodies still and both of their necks at odd angles. She held Ben by the throat, his feet kicking in the air.

"You insult Avien'zia by claiming to be a hunter of men in her name. I should snap your fool neck and drop you at the gates of her temple."

Ben wheezed and clawed at her hand to no effect.

"But that is not what I have planned for you. Instead, you will tell these Orange Hounds that the title of bounty hunter is not to be taken by common thieves and cutthroats. No matter how powerful you think you are, you are mice compared to those that truly worship the goddess of the hunt." She tossed him away like a child would discard an old toy. "Now run back to Lurthalan, dog, and tell whoever you call master that the will of the gods should still be feared and respected."

Ben struggled to his feet and shot Shayua a look that clearly conveyed his feelings towards her. Then he glanced at all of his fallen companions. His anger faltered and he hobbled off without another word. Leaving Ezzy with Shayua.

"You," the bounty hunter said, leveling a finger at Ezzy.

"What?" Ezzy tried her best to return the strong woman's gaze. Tried and failed.

"You came to my aid." Her voice was flat, not giving a hint if Shayua was appreciative or condemning. "Why?"

"I saw you as the lesser of two evils. As unpleasant as you have been, I figured you were a better captor than those men."

"And that is the only reason?"

"Maybe."

"Well, your reasons are your own, but your actions have created a problem."

"What kind of problem?"

"I have to accept that you may have saved my life, as I'm sure if those men had won the struggle they would have tortured me and then taken it."

"Um, ok. I'm not sure what to say."

"Neither do I. I have yet to decide what I am to do with you."

"Well, you could always let us go."

"The thought had crossed my mind. It would ease my--"

Shayua cut off as she lurched forward and crumpled to the ground. Nolan stood behind her, his walking staff gripped tightly in his hands.

"Should I hit her again?"

Chapter Fourteen

NEW UNDERSTANDINGS

Temple Bounty - 35 Silver (Alive)

Orange Hound Bounty - 60 Silver (Alive)

"I still think this is a bad idea."

Ezzy rolled her eyes, even though Nolan was walking behind her. They had had this conversation the previous night and again this morning when they awoke. Now, as they came to the end of another day of walking, he wanted to bring it up again? The man could be so frustrating.

"And I still say it was the only thing we could do."

"Not the only thing..."

"It was the only acceptable thing to do. Nolan, please don't start. We've been walking all day across the grasslands, I'm tired, and I'm certainly not going to change my mind now."

"Fine, fine. But you are going to have to let her go at some point."

"I know."

Coming to a stop, she turned to look at their prisoner. Shayua was draped over Paz's shoulder, her hands tied behind her back and her ankles bound. The cold, calculating look the bounty hunter was directing towards her though sent a chill down her spine. The woman hadn't said a single word the entire day. That stare was more than enough to express her feelings.

"I don't know what she'll do if we let her go."

"She'll probably take you over her knee and--"

"Me? You're the one that smacked her in the back of the head with your staff. I would think if she was mad at anyone, it would be you for blindsiding her."

"I'm not the one she's been shooting daggers at with her eyes."

"I know."

"And I'm not the one that's kept her tossed over Paz's back all day. I'm sure the jostling around hasn't been the most enjoyable traveling experience. Especially all bound up."

"I know, I know!"

With a thought, she had Paz drop their packs, then take Shayua in both hands and place her on her feet. Ezzy had her Vilathos keep a solid grip on the woman. Who knew what the trained bounty hunter could do, even properly tied up. By the gods, Ezzy hoped they had properly tied her up. Well, she would keep her distance and try to reason with the woman.

"Nolan, why don't you start setting up camp while I have a friendly conversation with our new traveling companion."

"Ok, but I'll be right here when she gets free and starts tossing you around."

Ignoring his comment, Ezzy walked up to the woman, keeping out of easy reach just in case Shayua somehow got free. Nolan was right, they had to work things out. Better now than later.

"Ok, it's getting late and I'm sure you don't want to sleep wrapped around my Vilathos's shoulders. Can we come to some kind of understanding?"

Shayua continued to stare at her for quite some time, then finally looked away. "Yes."

Well, that was a good sign.

"I want to let you go, but I can't have you turning around and knocking Nolan and me senseless."

"That is not my plan."

"Well, would you be so kind as to let me know what you're planning?"

"No."

Throwing her hands in the air, Ezzy began to pace in front of the woman.

"How do you expect me to let you go if you won't tell me what you are going to do? What am I even saying? How could I even know if what you tell me is the truth? You might say we should call things even, and then as soon as you are untied, turn on us."

"I do not lie. If I said I was going to let you go, I would."

"So, you are willing to let us go?"

"I don't know yet."

"You are the definition of frustrating! Can you tell me anything?"

"I have no intention of hurting you or the old man. But I will stay with you until I figure out what is the right thing for me to do."

"Well, that's a start. Anything else?"

"You frustrate me. I do not know what to do with you."

"Good! Then at least you know how I feel. How about this, if I let you go, do you swear not to attack us in our sleep?"

"That I can do."

"And after all your talk of honor, I know you wouldn't go back on your word."

Shayua's lip curled downward, exposing more of her sharp teeth.

"I'll take that as a yes. I'm still going to have Paz hold on to your weapons though. Now here, turn around so I can untie your hands."

"That won't be necessary."

Shayua brought her hands forward, the untied rope dangling from her wrist. She knelt down and started working on the binds around her ankles, as calm as if she were lacing her boots. When she was free, she stood back up and gave Ezzy a quizzical look.

"So, what now?"

"Um, well, now I guess we settle in for the night. Have something to eat. We'll want our energy for tomorrow. We should reach the north side of Rensen forest, and then it will be slow going since we won't be taking the road."

"Good. I will cook."

"Oh well, you don't have to do that..."

But the woman was already moving. She strode past Nolan, who raised his walking staff in a defensive manner. She ignored him.

"Do you have kindling gathered? I did not see you picking up material as you traveled."

"Yes," Nolan said, still brandishing his staff in her direction. "We had a supply already. It's behind the bag holding our cooking pot."

"Thank you."

While Nolan stood in shocked silence, Ezzy moved to the woman's side. She pulled out the pot and its stand while Shayua started building a fire. Nolan might not be able to handle surprises, but Ezzy was more adaptable. Plus, having the woman cook for them, instead of knocking them around, was a much better option.

"So, Shayua, that's an interesting name."

"Do not ask about my past. It will prevent unpleasant situations."

"I wasn't trying to," Shay turned and gave her a pointed look. "Okay, maybe I was, but it's just I've never seen anyone like you before."

"I'm sure a girl that grew up in a situation like yours has not seen a lot of the world."

"What is that supposed to mean?"

"Esmerelda Ciantar, daughter of Meganan Ciantar and Alexia Ciantar, siblings Maxanan and Moxanan, one of the oldest Hawkpurse families in recorded history." She spoke as if she was reading from a history book. "Bonded to a Vilathos by Nolan

Bintershad. Trained in hand-to-hand combat. Willful and stubborn. Father deceased, murdered in the Deadlands, family home burned down, probably by a rival family--"

"Stop!" Ezzy had heard enough. Her father's death and the downfall of her family were not things that should be checked off of a list. "You know nothing about who I am or what I've been through. You know nothing of the stresses and dangers of being a Hawkpurse. You're just a bounty hunter, responsible for nobody but yourself."

For a moment, Ezzy thought she had gone too far. Shayua stared back at her with a blank expression. Her dark grey eyes seemed to probe Ezzy to her very soul. Tensing, she expected the woman to lash out. Instead, she got laughed at.

"That is true," she said, laughing lightly. It was a strange sound to hear from the serious woman. "I haven't suffered the same life you have. I presumed too much, and it is clear what I learned about you does not match what I have seen. Except perhaps the part about being stubborn."

Was that a joke? Shayua had stopped laughing. The blasted woman was impossible to read.

"Yes, well, I am sure there are a lot of different stories about my family, just as there are about the other Hawkpurse families."

"Perhaps. I've never hunted a member of a Hawkpurse family before. If I may be so bold to ask, what has driven you to a life of crime? Surely you had some money put away even after everything that happened."

"What? I'm not a criminal."

"You have a bounty on your head. That makes you a criminal."

"No, that's just a misunderstanding--"

"How do you misunderstand the willful destruction of property?"

"It was in self-defense. I was ambushed by those Orange Hound fellows. Not the ones we saw, but a group of them in Halyquain. I had Paz give them a sound beating; it just happened that some nearby buildings were damaged in the process."

"I saw no mention of any of this in the bounty."

"Of course not. From what I've heard, the gangs run things in Halyquain. I'm sure they twisted the story around, especially if they are holding some kind of grudge against me."

Shayua spit on the ground. It was disgusting, but before Ezzy could call her out on her behavior, the bounty hunter spoke.

"A corrupted bounty. These Orange Hounds spit in the very face of Avien'zia. Why the goddess has not struck all of them down is beyond me."

"That's exactly what I was thinking." At least she was now.

Shayua grew silent for a moment as she used a rock and piece of flint to light the brush and get the fire going. When she had built the flame up, it made her eyes sparkle in the fading light of the evening.

"Esmerelda," she said, her tone all business. "I have decided to reject your bounty. I will not take you back to Lurthalan."

"Thank you, Shayua. That's a relief to hear."

"You travel to Shade now, correct? I will go with you."

"Um..." The last thing Nolan and Ezzy needed was a hot-headed bounty hunter following them around. Especially one that stood out as much as Shayua. Now, how to reject her in the nicest way possible? "That is very generous of you to offer to protect us, but with Paz I really don't see the need..."

Shayua barked a laugh. "I am not coming along to protect you. Those Orange Hounds need to die for the mockery they made of my goddess and their corruption of my profession. I would be insulting my goddess if I allow them to live. Since they seem most interested in you, I will have the best chance to kill more of them if I stay by your side."

"Now wait a minute, you can't just use us as bait."

"I don't know," Nolan cut in. "Those Orange Hounds are going to be after us anyway. One more set of eyes, especially attached to someone as skilled as Shayua, would certainly help."

"Paz can handle..."

"Paz didn't stop Shayua from getting the drop on us."

"This arguing is pointless," Shayua said as she placed their pot over the fire. "I wasn't asking permission to accompany you. I simply told you I was coming. It's not up for discussion."

"I could just as easily have Paz toss you over his shoulder again."

"And eventually you would let me go again." She pulled a few pieces of jerky out and tossed it into the pot, then began to cut up a potato from their supply of food. "Either way I will be with you as you travel. Best to let me use my own feet and not monopolize your monster's arms."

Shayua was right. As much as Ezzy hated to admit it. Her "stubborn side," though, wanted to have Paz show her who was in charge here. Maybe another day of being tossed over its back would teach her a thing or two. Probably not, though. Getting on the woman's good side was a better idea. Ezzy had a brief flash of the bounty hunter standing over the dead gang members. Definitely better to be on her good side. That didn't mean giving in nicely.

"Just finish cooking. If you are going to stay with us, you need to pull your weight."

Good job, Ezzy, you told her.

She didn't let Shayua's laughter diminish her sense of authority one bit.

Chapter Fifteen

A DEAL STRUCK

Ezzy had enjoyed the spicy seasonings Shayua used in her cooking. The blend of sweet and spicy flavors Shayua had added to the meal made even the normally bland rabbit stew taste like a meal created in the finest of inns. Ezzy had lain down for the night full and content, and although she would never admit it, she did feel safer with Shayua there.

And then she awoke with her stomach screaming at her. The rest of her night was spent in the fetal position while her companions slept peacefully. After a night of a war raging in her stomach, Ezzy decided that Shayua could pull her weight doing something other than cooking for the group.

When the sun finally started to rise, she felt exhausted. She stayed in her blankets while the others packed things up. At one point, Shayua made some unflattering remarks about her laziness, which motivated her to finally get moving. How the woman could constantly eat food with those spices and still function was beyond her. And how had Nolan gotten a good night's sleep as well? She had expected his constitution to be the weakest out of the three of them. Apparently the man had an iron stomach. Not wanting to look like a wimp, Ezzy mustered her strength and kept from complaining as they headed out.

Trees started to speckle the land at first as they moved south, interrupting the plains that they had been traveling over for the last few days. Then the trees grew thicker as they found the true edge of the forest towards the end of the afternoon. With all of the logging limited to the west side of the Melcoi River, the forest was slowly spreading north on this side. The section where the road ran through was supposed to be relatively clear, but they had chosen to enter the woods much father east. The bounty hunter had been annoyed by the decision but hadn't argued with it. Much.

As they began making their way through the forest, Ezzy couldn't help but wonder about their strange new companion. She had met a few bounty hunters in her time, but Shayua was like none she had ever met before. And it wasn't just because of her extraordinary appearance. Any bounty hunter hired by Ezzy's father had been a mixture of cockiness and abrasiveness. All they had cared about was the money her father promised to pay them. There had been a few times that Ezzy had snuck out of her room to hear her father arguing with a bounty hunter over a botched job or a mark that had turned up dead instead of captured. Those didn't seem to follow this code that Shayua had mentioned, although they all claimed to follow Avien'zia.

Shayua was different. Going by her actions and what she said, Shayua took her role as a bounty hunter seriously and the rules involved as law. Ezzy didn't know much about Avien'zia, but it seemed that Shayua's devotion to her goddess was absolute. Which made the fact that the woman had given up on her bounty all the more confusing. Wouldn't the deliberate refusal to complete a bounty anger the goddess? Had her decision been based on some side of Avien'zia that Ezzy didn't know, or did it have something to do with where she came from? It was frustrating to realize that she knew so little about Avien'zia and many of the other deities and their practices. And she couldn't ask the woman about her heritage. Ezzy would have to try a different tactic with the woman to get some answers.

As they trudged their way through the forest, stepping around trees and saplings or pushing through dense overgrowth, Ezzy tried to think of the best way to get the woman to open up. In the end, she decided to on focus on her bounty hunter aspect and see if that made her open up more about her religion.

"So, how long have you been a bounty hunter?"

Shayua stepped around a sapling before replying. "I started training when I was eight and took my first contract when I was fifteen. So since my first contract, it's been ten years."

"You started training at the age of eight?"

"Yes, my mother bought me an apprenticeship through the temple."

"And that's normal?"

"Why wouldn't it be?" Her voice grew cold.

"I don't know, I meant no offense." Ezzy brushed a branch out of her way to give her time to choose her next words. "I know very little about Avien'zia's temple. I've spent most of my life devoted mostly to Drenks, but with everything that's happened to my family, I no longer pray to him. Since I started looking for the person or people responsible for my family's downfall, I've been considering giving my prayers to Avien'zia."

"You have abandoned your patron deity?" She made it sound like Ezzy had slaughtered a whole village.

"He has abandoned me and my family! My family devoted decades in service to him, and now we've been torn down to nothing. All because of the actions of one man. Either that one man was more powerful than a god or my god abandoned my family first."

Ezzy hadn't meant to raise her voice. She never *intended* to get upset when she thought about what happened to her family. Her emotions were like a pile of tinder sitting next to a candle. All it took was the smallest push to knock that candle over and start a blaze. Struggling to get her temper under control, she took out her aggression on a nearby plant, trampling it under her boot. Shayua grew quiet for a moment. When she finally spoke, her tone had changed. It sounded...understanding.

"If what you say is true, I understand why you would disregard such a fickle deity. So, you wish to follow Avien'zia now because..."

"I want to hunt down the man that caused all of it. I want to bring him to justice. And I'm willing to do whatever it takes to accomplish that goal."

Shayua stopped and spun around so suddenly that Ezzy put her arms up in defense. The bounty hunter gripped Ezzy's shoulders with her strong hands and looked directly into her eyes.

"Esmerelda Ciantar. I understand now why I found your bounty. Why I felt the desire not to complete it. Avien'zia must have put me on the path to you for a higher cause."

"Oh?" Ezzy had no idea what the woman was talking about. She kept quiet and waited to see where this was going.

"You have prayed to Avien'zia, yes? Prayed for help in finding this man?"

"Almost every day."

"I believe your prayers have been answered. Avien'zia has placed me in your life to see if you are worthy of her blessings. I will join your hunt. Train you. Test you. Make you a true hunter of men. This man and all men will come to fear Esmerelda Ciantar even more than her metal monster."

"Ezzy," Nolan cut in, "I don't think--"

"You don't need to think, Thaljori, as this decision is out of your hands. It's out of all of our hands. It clearly is the will of the goddess." Returning her attention to Ezzy, Shayua's grip on her shoulders tightened to the point of being almost painful. "You must see that this is what is supposed to happen, yes?"

"I don't know. It's hard to believe a goddess would take a personal interest in me..."

"That is because you are used to following a god that sits back and lets his worshippers send him praises for boons he has not caused and blames others for their failures. Your former god sits and eats and grows fat with overindulgence while his followers battle it out for even the smallest scraps of his attention. Avien'zia watches out for her people. She makes our arrows fly true. Allows us to hear the slightest rustle of an animal we hunt. Shows our eyes even the smallest tracks while in pursuit of our bounties."

"I haven't noticed any of this since I started praying--"

Shayua released her shoulders and stepped back.

"Giving her lip service and asking for favors does not make you a true servant of Avien'zia. Many hunters of either men or animals make the same mistake, either from ignorance or laziness. Those willing to listen to the sermon of her Voice, decipher their true meanings, and follow their instructions are the ones that become close to the goddess."

"And you're willing to teach me what it means to follow her completely? To gain the heightened senses and abilities?"

Ezzy wasn't sure if she believed everything Shayua was saying, but it had captured her interest. Did the deities of their realm exert more of their influence than she had been led to believe? Even if half of what she said was true, the chance to gain Shayua's skills would be hard to pass up. Especially combined with her control of Paz.

"I can teach you how to hunt and fight, how to live in a way Avien'zia would find pleasing. Whether she takes an interest, no one can say. We cannot begin to comprehend the thoughts of the gods."

"Please teach me, Shayua." Nolan let out a snort behind her but she ignored it. "I want to learn."

"Do not ask for this so eagerly. You need to understand something before you make any commitment to this life. If I'm to instruct you, that means you must follow my instructions and orders. The man that trained me was a harsh and unforgiving mentor. There were days I wanted to kill him, but I humbled myself and followed his instructions to the letter. I would be doing him and Avien'zia an injustice if I expected any less from you. I will not waste my time if you are only going to follow what I say when it is convenient for you."

"I will follow your instructions on the condition they don't interfere with my plans of finding justice for my father."

Another snort from Nolan. The man needed to keep his opinions to himself. She could follow orders when she agreed to it. If everything Shayua was saying was true, she would gratefully swallow her pride to have even the slightest advantage of catch this Ean Sangrave.

"Can I ask questions?" Ezzy continued.

"Questions are not a problem. I expect you to have many questions about what we do. It's defiance that won't be tolerated."

"I swear, Shayua, I won't let you down. Train me."

The grin that appeared on Shayua's face was solemn.

"Excellent. May Avien'zia smile on us both this day. Now, hold out your hand."

Ezzy did as she was told then pulled it back as Shayua pulled out one of her many knives. That earned her a growl from the woman.

"An agreement this important must be made in blood, Esmerelda. Avien'zia would be content with nothing less."

"How much blood?"

"Hold on," Nolan said, limping over to stand almost between the two women. "This is going too far."

"This is no concern of yours, Thaljori." Shayua went to push him out of the way but he raised his staff and pointed it at her face.

"Ezzy is more of a concern of mine than she is of yours. You've had your turn to speak, now she will hear what I have to say."

He turned his back on Shayua, something Ezzy would never have done after threatening the massive woman, and raised his free hand in a soothing manner.

"I understand you want to find this Ean fellow and bring him to justice for what he did to your family. Believe me, I want to see the same thing. Your father was one of the few people I could call a friend."

He placed a gentle hand on her shoulder and pulled her closer, his voice dropping to a whisper.

"But I'm scared this path will lead you down a dark path. You already hold so much anger. I'm afraid learning to follow a goddess that gets a thrill out of a hunt and killing will just make that anger settle deeper inside you. Left unchecked, it will consume you. I won't let that happen."

His fears were unnecessary, of course, but his words were still appreciated. After all this was said and done, she would make sure that her friend was well taken care of for the rest of his life. Even if she was the one that had to do it.

"You're overreacting, Nolan. She's offering me a way to take better care of myself. I hate to admit it, but you know those rabbits I said I caught a few days ago?

Well, I actually got them from--"

"Yes, yes, I figured you bought them. You're not really listening to what I'm saying..."

"You're worried that I'll become some killing machine. I get it. It's not going to happen, Nolan. Plus, I have you around to keep me grounded."

"I won't always be around, Ezzy."

"Why would you say something like that? Ok, never mind, I don't want to talk about it. I'm going to train with Shayua. My decision is final."

"Stubborn girl..." Nolan mumbled as he stalked away as fast as his injured leg could carry him. Ezzy took a step to go after him, but Shayua stuck out an arm to block her path.

"Let him go. You are an adult and must make your own decisions. He either will accept it or not. Now hold out your hand."

Ezzy did as she was told. When Shayua placed the blade of the knife across her palm, fear almost made her pull her hand back again. What was she getting herself into? Then she pictured her father. The last time she had seen him. Hugging him good-bye, not knowing it was for the last time. She steeled her resolve.

Her hand trembled as Shayua grasped her wrist. As much as Ezzy wanted to put on a brave face, when the blade cut into her skin, she cried out in pain. Shayua squeezed her wrist a few times until the blood dribbled down her hand. Then the bounty hunter cut into her own hand, took Ezzy's hand in her own, and squeezed even harder.

"A deal struck."

With that, Shayua nodded and stepped back.

"Wait... that's it?"

"You expected more?"

"Well... yes! I expected some big speech or proclamation to your goddess."

"OUR goddess.'

"Yes, of course that's what I meant, but I just thought--"

"Our goddess does not require big, elaborate rituals like other deities. Avien'zia is more about action over words."

"Oh, well, let's get started then. I want to learn everything."

"In time. At this moment we should fix your hand. I won't be able to teach you to use a bow if your palm gets infected."

"True. I should wash the wound and get it wrapped."

"That won't be necessary."

Shayua pulled a small vial from her pouch and popped off the cork.

"Let me see your hand."

Shayua gripped her wrist again, and sprinkled a ground-up powder over the wound. She then used her free hand to rub it in. It hurt at first, but then the sharp pain turned into a light throbbing. A few moments later it was gone completely.

"What was that?"

"Rottwealth."

"Rottwealth? Just that small amount costs a fortune!"

"Not as much as it used to cost. The supply in Lurthalan has increased this past year."

"Still, for you to use it on me..."

"As my student, you are my responsibility now. To let something bad happen, even something as small as an infected hand, would reflect poorly on me. I've taken on a great responsibility becoming your mentor."

"Shayua, I had no idea."

"Well, let this be your first lesson. Everything you do from this point on is a reflection of how I instruct you. You can thank me for mentoring you by trying your best not to embarrass me."

"Thank you."

"Good. I'm hoping to at least make it a few days before I have to administer your first beating."

"First?"

Oh, Ezzy. What have you gotten yourself into?

Chapter Sixteen

AWAKENING

"Wake up," Shayua's grating voice tore Ezzy out of a pleasant dream that included a bathhouse, a handsome masseur, and his magical fingers along her spine. "We have a lot to do before we head out."

Ezzy's body ached and her eyes fought her as she tried to open them. They had stayed up late, Shayua wanting to teach her how to shoot a bow by fire and moonlight. The woman hadn't let Ezzy sleep until she had fired three shots with acceptable form. All she had to eat were a few pieces of jerky, thankfully spice-free. The three moons had all been floating in the sky by the time Ezzy was allowed to lie down. It had taken even longer for her to fall asleep as she tossed and turned on the various rocks and roots that made up the forest floor.

And now she was being woken up in the last remaining moments of night when the moons were gone and dawn was just starting to peek over the Unyielding Wall.

"Just a few more moments," she replied.

That earned her a kick in the side that almost knocked the air from her lungs.

"The sun will not wait a few more moments for you to rise. We go by its schedule, not yours, Esmerelda."

"Understood," Ezzy wheezed. Climbing out of her blankets, she let her eyes adjust to the dark. Nolan was still sleeping, one hand resting on his staff. The man was snoring, which bothered her for some reason.

"Come. This way."

Shayua was a blur of movement in the darkness. Ezzy followed in silence, wondering what morning activity the bounty hunter had planned. More practice with a bow in low light? Maybe some hunting and trapping practice? What else could they do this early in the morning?

I hope this isn't an everyday thing. Wait, where did Shayua go?

Lost in thought, Ezzy had lost track of the woman. The woods were so dark. The only thing her senses could pick up was the snap of branches and twigs beneath her feet as she stumbled forward. She might as well have been wandering blind. Part of her wanted to call out for her mentor, but her pride kept her quiet. She would just stumble on until the woman called for her or the sun came up enough for her to see.

"This way, little rabbit."

Shayua's voice came from behind her, possibly on her right side. How had the woman gotten behind her?

"Which way?"

"Over here."

Orienting herself in the direction of the voice, Ezzy set off in the new direction. The bounty hunter's reasons for getting her up this early had better be more than to have her traipse about lost in the woods. If the only lesson she was supposed to learn was how inept she was in the dark...well, there wasn't much she could do. Maybe toss out Shayua's spices so the woman couldn't continue to poison--

A snapping sound came from her right, followed by the sound of something falling through the trees. Before she could react, something gripped her ankle and pulled her legs out from under her. Her back and head hit the ground hard and then she was lifted into the air feet first. Her vision swam from the impact on the ground and her arms hung limply just above the ground as she swung upside-down. A hand gripped her shirt and Shayua was kneeling right in her face, their noses almost touching.

"Seems like you're caught in a snare, little rabbit."

"I don't see how swinging from my ankles helps me get closer to Avien'zia."

"Oh, but it does." The slow scrape of a knife leaving its sheath sent a chill down Ezzy's spine. The cold look in Shayua's eyes made Ezzy tense up even more. "The capture of prey, offered up to Avien'zia, is a great compliment to our goddess."

This close, Shayua's lower incisors looked like little daggers sticking up over her lip. And where was the knife she had heard come free?

"Shayua, I'm not prey. You said yourself you had abandoned the bounty."

"This is true, but it does not mean I cannot still hunt you for sport. And now that I've caught you, I can offer our goddess a tribute of blood."

"Shayua, this isn't funny anymore. You're starting to sca--"

Ezzy's voice cut off with a squeak as the blade of a knife touched her neck.

"A morning offering of blood was how I first introduced myself properly to the goddess, Esmerelda. I believe your blood will be an acceptable greeting to her again."

"Shayua, please..." Fear gripped her. She tried to summon Paz to her but all her focus was on the sharp edge pressed against her skin.

"Please? You want to just get right to it? I like that."

The blade began to move.

"No!"

Ezzy closed her eyes as a sharp pain rippled through her.

And then it was gone.

Her own hands went right to her throat, feeling along the skin for where the knife had done its damage. Confusion sank in as she failed to find even a scratch. As her mind struggled to understand what was happening, a dull ache started on the left side of her head. Her hand moved to the source of the pain, her ear, and she felt something wet. Daring to open her eyes, she looked at the small amount of blood smeared on her hand. Then she saw Shayua sitting a few paces away barely in sight.

The woman was smiling!

Not the smile of a psychopath. Not a condescending smirk. The bounty hunter wore a wide grin, her eyes filled with nothing but warmth.

"Shayua! By the Abyss, I thought you were going to slit my throat. You could have said all you were going to do was nick my ear."

"Where would be the fun in that?"

"So that's what you consider fun? Making someone nearly wet themselves?"

"Were you close? That would have made the joke even better."

"Shayua…"

"I told you yesterday that to allow anything horrible to happen to you would reflect poorly on me. That especially includes killing you."

"The words seem less true when you have a knife to my throat."

"That's only because you understand nothing about our goddess. But you will learn."

"Can I learn while standing on my own two feet? All the blood is rushing to my head, and I'm starting to get a little woozy."

Shayua gripped something at her side and pulled. The tension of the rope holding her up disappeared and Ezzy dropped to the ground. She barely tucked in time to avoid landing on her head, her back taking the brunt of the fall instead. An exposed root dug into her ribs, making her grunt as she tried to sit up. Keeping her discomfort to herself, she instead focused on removing the rope from around her ankles. When she finished, Shayua motioned for her to move closer. Ezzy crawled over and took a seat directly in front of her. To her credit, when Shayua then held out a knife, Ezzy did not shy away

"This is my Korin. Hold it."

Ezzy did as she was told, taking the blade in her hand. The handle felt awkward, brown leather wrapped around whatever material made up the grip, and it was clearly meant for someone with a larger hand than her own. It had no hand guard or fancy decorations. The most interesting part about it was the blade. The dark gray color of it threw her off for a moment, but she guessed it was made of bone. Her own blood still adorned the tip. Overall it was an unimpressive weapon and certainly not something she would have thought had special meaning.

"I don't understand. Is there something I'm missing? It seems like a something put together with scraps."

"You are not far off. I made it solely from what I harvested from my very first hunt and kill."

Ezzy quickly handed it back.

"You mean, it's made from the parts of a person?" To think the bone came from a human was gross enough, but to think of how she had made the leather of the handle...

"No, no, no. My first kill was a boar in these very woods."

"Oh well, that's a relief."

"Do not think that it has not been done before. My mentor's first kill in Avien'zia's name was a man. The target was a murderer of women and children, and my mentor took great joy in ridding him from the world. Having been born a weapon-smith's son, my mentor's blade was expertly made from the pieces of the man. If your first kill is a human, I will expect you to do the same."

"Really? That's horrendous!"

"So you would not do it?" The tone of Shayua's voice made her words more of an accusation than a question.

"I...will just make sure my first kill is an animal. Then it won't be an issue."

"We will see. Sometimes the decision to kill is made for you." Rising, Shayua sheathed her Korin. "Congratulations, my apprentice. You have taken your first steps in truly knowing your goddess."

"Really? Just a little bloodletting? Should I feel different?"

"You *are* different. You are just too blind to see it."

"What's that supposed to mean?"

"It means, all you have to do is open your eyes."

"Stop talking in riddles. My eyes are open."

"Then look around."

"What do you think I'm doing? All I see are trees and plants, a few birds perched in the trees around us. That smug look on your face."

"And how are you seeing all this without any light?"

"What? I...oh my..."

Shayua was right. The sun had yet to climb over the Wall. Even the dull glow of dawn hadn't appeared. And yet she could see everything around her. Could make out details where she should only be able to see subtle blurs. Thinking back, Ezzy realized that she had been able to tell Shayua's expressions and see all of the details of her Korin with little light penetrating the canopy of the forest. She had been too foolish to realize it.

Her mind reeled at the implications. It was all true! Ezzy twirled around, trying to see as much as she could in the darkness. The realization that her new vision only penetrated a few paces away diminished her excitement, but only by a small amount. The fact that she could see clearly any distance at all was amazing. And all of this had come within the first day!

"Is this what you meant? Can you see in the dark as well?"

"Yes."

"This is amazing. It's such a gift."

"It is not a gift, Esmerelda. It is a borrowed skill. You are Avien'zia's now. She can provide you with such skills as long as you follow her ways. With time and devotion, they can improve. If you displease her, she will cast you aside and you will lose it all. Do you understand?"

"Yes, you've made it perfectly clear."

"Good. Then let's head back. I want Nolan awake and ready to move as soon as the sun finally gets around to rising."

"Sounds good to me. Oh, and Shayua, one last thing?"

"Yes?"

"You can just call me Ezzy."

Chapter Seventeen

LOST IN THOUGHT

They traveled through the woods for three days without incident, which should have made Nolan content, but he was worried that his brain was turning to mush. Ever since he had bonded Paz and Ezzy again, his equilibrium was off. Worse, he was having trouble concentrating. In the middle of a sentence, he would forget what he was talking about. He would have a useful thought, but it would evaporate before reaching his tongue. At least the trek had been peaceful. Considering it was the Chill season, the weather was unseasonably warm. At night, the blankets were enough to keep the cold at bay. That didn't mean he wasn't looking forward to a roof over his head and a warm bed. And a hearty meal in a tavern would be nice.

While Nolan appreciated Shayua's efforts to spice up their food, he had grown tired of eating road rations and rabbit meat. What he wouldn't do for a warm loaf of bread, a cup of spiced wine, and a comfy chair by the fire to enjoy them! Most of all, though, he wanted to get Ezzy alone for a few moments and away from her new "mentor."

The two women were walking in front of him at the moment, talking in low tones about who knew what. In only a few days, the two had become inseparable. Always talking about Avien'zia this and hunting that. Shayua never said very much about her goddess around him, which was fine as far as he saw it. Nolan was quite content following Ni'Aren. Knowledge. That's what was important in this world. Not the ability to catch and skin a rabbit. Ezzy had finally caught one the previous night, which he had to admit was impressive. And Shayua flavored them with some tasty spices...

Focus, Nolan.

Stopping for a moment, he rubbed at his left elbow. He had been lost in his own thoughts yesterday when he missed seeing the fallen log. He tried to walk right through it, tripped, and landed on the only jagged rock in the area. To make matters worse, he had gotten tangled up in a bush, and Ezzy had to have Paz pull him out. He didn't know what was worse, the nagging pain in his elbow or the annoyed grunts Shayua made sure Nolan heard whenever he had the least bit of trouble moving through the dense forest. Both made sleeping difficult. His elbow hurt whenever he rolled on it, and Shayua, well, she was a killer.

"Nolan!" Ezzy was yelling from far ahead of him. "You ok?"

How had she gotten so far ahead? Even Paz was ahead of him. He hadn't even noticed the Vilathos trudging past him, sticks and saplings crackling under its metal feet. He was getting lost in his thoughts more and more often. Deep in thought. And it was getting worse. Every time he used his power, it was like...well...

"Nolan!"

A hand on his shoulder startled Nolan out of his thoughts. He was even more startled to see Ezzy standing right in his face. Had the girl run back to him? Had she...

"Nolan. Focus. Focus on me."

He did. He looked at her young face, a few new wrinkles around her amber eyes. Eyes full of concern. She knew what was happening to him. He had warned her the same day she had asked him to come with her on this search for justice. Was it still justice she sought or was it revenge? Had it always been revenge? His biggest fear was that she--

Her hand struck his face. Not a hard slap, but it certainly had enough force to knock the thoughts from his head.

"You hit me!"

"I'm sorry! You weren't responding and I got worried."

"Yes, well, I understand. Thank you."

She let out a laugh. He knew her well enough to hear the nervousness she tried to hide in it.

"Anytime. I wish I could knock some sense into you more often." Her tone grew more serious and she dropped her voice. "It's getting worse, isn't it, Nolan? It took you a long time to wake up after the last time you bound me to Paz, and these last couple of days you've been quiet. More quiet than usual."

"It's becoming more difficult to get out of my own head, like my mind is a forest more dense than the one we're in, and I'm trying to find my way at night. Before, it came and went, but now..."

He grew silent as Shayua approached.

"Is everything alright?" The bounty hunter's eyes scanned him top to bottom. "Does the old man need a break? It would be a shame to stop now when we are so close to our destination."

"Nolan's fine, Shayua. His knee is just bothering him."

"Fine. I'm going to scout ahead then. After you have assisted the old man, catch up quick. We still have much I wish to discuss before we reach Shade."

"Of course, Shayua. I'll be there soon."

Nolan glared at the bounty hunter as she walked off. Why was she in charge now? This was Ezzy's hunt... Hunt? Wonderful, now he was talking like her too.

"I'll show you old, you towering red buffoon," he said, brandishing his staff at her back.

"I heard that, old man!"

"Good!"

"Nolan, stop." Ezzy put a hand on his arm and lowered it along with his staff. "You shouldn't say things about her skin. You know how much it upsets her."

"Let her be upset. She had no problem insulting me."

"True, but you couldn't rip off both her arms if you got angry enough. The same can't be said for her."

"Let her try. If you've already forgotten, I was the one to capture her in the first place."

"You struck her from behind after she was about to thank me for helping her."

"Don't make excuses for her."

Rolling her eyes, Ezzy put an arm around his shoulder and started leading him forward. "Come on, let's get going. We can walk and talk for a bit."

"I don't need a babysitter, Ezzy. I'm more than twenty years your senior"

"You're also my friend and I worry about you. So humor me."

"Fine, but we're not going to talk about my...condition."

"Of course we are," she said with a laugh. Nolan tried to glare at her, but the sound of her laughter broke his resolve. He let a smile touch his lips, but didn't give her the satisfaction of laughing with her.

"You are impossible, Ezzy."

"Yes, but you've known that since the day you made me that first Vilathos doll."

He couldn't help but laugh again at the memory. She had been so excited by the gift, a small doll made mostly of cloth and straw. When he had bonded her to it, even with the magic strengthening the material, it could barely stand on its own. By the end of the day though, she had it tumbling around and making human gestures. Ezzy had always been a natural at controlling Vilathos. That had been the deciding factor when she had begged him to bond her to Paz. She had been so desperate that day. It broke his heart to see her--

Nolan's foot struck something and he pitched forward. He felt Ezzy's arm try to keep him upright, but he ended up dragging her down as well. She let out a yelp as they tumbled forward landed in a heap. Nolan lost his grip on his staff as he hit the ground and the dull throb of his previous injuries doubled in intensity from the impact. Once the initial shock of hitting the ground wore off, they disentangled from each other and climbed back onto their feet.

"Well, that was embarrassing," Ezzy said, brushing leaves and twigs off her yellow cloak.

"At least your new mentor is out of sight. I'm sure she would have loved to point and laugh at the two of us."

"Oh, give her a chance, Nolan. She's going to be with us for a while. You might as well try to be friendly."

"I'll leave that to you. Meanwhile I'll stick to my job of trying to keep you out of trouble."

"Need I remind you who just made both of us fall?"

"Right, because you've never tripped before."

Her voice grew serious as she looked him directly in the eyes. "Nolan, I know it wasn't clumsiness that made you fall. You were laughing along with me one moment and then you suddenly stopped. Your eyes glazed over. I literally watched as you disappeared into your own head."

"Ezzy, I really don't want to talk about it. I'm just tired. I need a night in a real bed, in a warm room, after a very large meal. Then I'll be fine."

"We both know you won't be fine."

"Just let it go for now, ok Ezzy? I promise if you want to talk about it, we can, once we get to Shade."

Frowning, she stared at him for a few moments. Nolan felt a swell of happiness at her obvious concern. He had always cared about Ezzy, ever since he became a permanent employee for the Ciantar family. After the death of her father, he had felt like he was becoming a father figure to the young woman. It was both intimidating and an honor. He had to make sure to live up to that title.

He had a few titles now. Thaljori was the major one. Follower of Ni'Aren was another. Shut-in was how his neighbors viewed him. Well, until he had started traipsing about looking...

Pull it together!

When his eyes focused again, he found Ezzy staring at him, the frown replaced with a sad smile. In the fading light, it was hard to make out the rest of her expression... fading light... wasn't it before midday? How long did each mental lapse last? They couldn't possibly have been walking all day already...

"Well," Ezzy's voice matched the sadness in her eyes. "It looks like you pulled yourself out of that little mental episode by yourself. I guess we can wait a bit to have a serious conversation about what's happening to you. We certainly won't be able to get far with you continuing to disappear. Maybe you are right and a good night's sleep in a warm bed will help your condition a little."

"Thank you, Ezzy. I appreciate it."

"As long as you realize that by a 'bit,' I mean the first day after we get settled into an inn and you get some rest."

"Fine, fine." He flashed her a small smile. "As long as you realize that the following morning I plan on sleeping in until lunch time."

"Sounds good to me." Ezzy gave him one last look over and then started walking ahead. After a few paces, she looked back over her shoulder at him. "That will give Shayua and me some time to hunt down this Saniteal we're looking for and politely ask him a few questions."

Nolan wasn't sure if it was the mischievous smile she wore or the inflection of her voice, but he knew right then that there was no way he would be sleeping in any time soon.

Chapter Eighteen

TWO SIDES OF A COIN

They reached Shade the following morning. As they approached their destination and the Unyielding Wall, Nolan noticed a slight change in the trees around them. The foliage seemed to bend and curve away from the wall, the trunks leaning away from the massive shadow cast by the wall. Their leaves, which should have already fallen once the Chill season began, were a mixture of bright green and purple. The closer they got to the wall, the more noticeable the change became. It made Nolan uncomfortable for some reason, and he was glad when the trees finally tapered off and the village of Shade spread out in front of them.

Shade was an average-sized village of a hundred or so residents. Consisting mostly of homes, the only shops entailed an inn, blacksmith, healer's hut, and general store. Nolan had never been there before, but he had read about it while working for Ezzy's father. It had been founded and was under the control of the Janpair Hawkpurse family. They had settled this close to the wall to have easy access to the unique worms that lived in the swamps to the south. Those worms produced a fine silk that couldn't be found anywhere else in the realm and made the most exquisite clothes and sheets. Nolan had two robes made of the material, his favorite, hanging back in his house. After he had bought his first, he had researched as much as he could about Shade and the nearby swamps. It had been done on a whim, but perhaps that information would prove useful while they were here.

With no point in worrying about being followed now, the three companions and Paz moved onto the road and walked into town. Their first destination was the village inn, The Cozy Shade, which was the first building sitting alongside the road to their left. A large two-story building with a stable that wrapped around behind it, the Cozy Shade was painted an obnoxious orange and green. The sign hanging out front was a detailed depiction of the Unyielding Wall behind a few buildings with the sun barely peeking over the top. It struck Nolan as strange to have such a detailed sign when few people actually visited the out-of-the-way village.

"What an ugly building," Ezzy said. "Why in the world would you paint anything, let alone an entire building, such a brash combination of colors?"

"Your father used to say that the people who live in Shade were a little... different."

"Well, I've met some of the cousins of the Janpair family, and if they were any indication of what the rest of this village is like, we are in for an entertaining couple of days."

"Who cares what the people are like," Shayua cut in. "I want some real meat, a good pig leg, or deer haunch. Anything that takes me more than two bites to finish."

"For once I agree with our tall tag-a-long," Nolan replied. "Sitting in a room with a toasty fire, a plate full of food, and a relaxing drink sounds perfect."

"And I agree with you, old man. Plentiful food AND drink are just rewards after days stumbling through the woods."

Ezzy rolled her eyes. "I'll be happy to be around people other than you two bickering children. That's the first thing you've agreed on the entire trip."

"We're older than you," both Shayua and Nolan said in unison. Nolan frowned as he realized what happened while Shayua just stormed off towards the inn.

"The two of you are ridiculous," Ezzy said before walking off towards the inn as well. Paz started moving immediately after her.

Watching Ezzy and her Vilathos walk off, Nolan had to admit that the comments between himself and the bounty hunter were unnecessary. He used to have better control over his words. Ni'Aren taught patience and to think before you spoke, but he often found himself doing the opposite. Plus, the woman had more than made up for trying to take them back to Lurthalan over the past couple of days. She supplemented their supplies of food, cooked amazing meals with the barest of supplies, and most importantly, offered them a great deal more protection than Nolan could provide.

Of course, in his mind, none of that compared to the negative influence she was having over Ezzy. When boiled down to the most basic facts, the only thing keeping him from accepting her was an unwavering fear that the woman would lead Ezzy down a darker path. She was smart, if a bit unpredictable, and she knew the difference between right and wrong. He had to hope it was possible Ezzy's newfound devotion to a goddess would not lead her to murder the man she was looking for.

And if Shayua and her cursed goddess did push her towards killing the man, Nolan would intervene and make her do what was right. No matter what the cost.

A cold wind brought him back to the here and now. Pulling his coat tighter against his body, he made his way to the inn. A fence built to contain the horses belonging to the inn's customers ran around the right side of the inn. Paz stood inside it, stoic and waiting for orders. It no longer held all of their bags, meaning Shayua and Ezzy must have already taken them inside. With thoughts of a warm room and meal driving him on, Nolan walked up the couple of steps to the front door and entered the inn.

Warmth greeted him like an old friend as soon as he stepped through the double doors, and he sighed as the chill immediately left his bones. Even the knife wound in his shoulder didn't throb as much as it had while they traveled. That alone was worth any amount of coin they would have to pay to stay here. Add in an evening by the fire to take some of the pain out of his aching knee and elbow, and he might even be able to sleep comfortably tonight.

The common room itself was almost empty. A single waitress moved about, pushing in stools and chairs and wiping down tables. A few patrons sat scattered about the room, enjoying a late breakfast or asleep with their heads on the table from the night before. None of those at the tables were Ezzy, but he did find Shayua sitting by the fire, a mug already in her hand. She frowned when she noticed him looking at her. Then, to his surprise, she waved him over.

"Esmerelda...I mean Ezzy, has already gotten us a room. She is taking our things up to it as we speak."

"That's good. I'm looking forward to a night in an actual bed."

"You don't like me."

The statement caught him off guard. Well, the woman was direct. He had to give her that.

"I don't like how much influence you're exerting over Ezzy."

"Ezzy is old enough to make her own decisions."

"Yes, you keep saying that, but age does not always bring wisdom. What you have to remember is that Ezzy grew up in one of the richest households in the realm. She was sheltered from the reality of our realm and is still learning how harsh and unforgiving this world really is. In that aspect she still is like a child. A very impressionable child."

"All the more reason for me to be her instructor. After all these years, it doesn't seem like you've done much to educate her about how to navigate Ven Khilada. Her first thought when a problem arises is to throw some money at it."

Nolan held back the biting retort that almost leapt out of his mouth. As much as he hated to admit it, Shayua was right. He had let her get away with a great deal. As much as he talked about keeping her head on straight, he never actually pushed his ideas on her. By the Abyss, he hadn't really impressed upon her how much he disliked her current path. He was taking the roundabout way by talking to Shayua instead of her. Worst of all, he couldn't think of a valid argument against what she said.

"That may be true," he finally admitted, "but I don't want her education to include murder and revenge. Ezzy already has a great deal of pent-up anger over what happened to her family. All it will take is a little push to change her hunt for justice to one of revenge."

"Is that what you think I'm teaching her? To seek revenge and kill those that have wronged her?"

"Isn't that what your goddess wishes?"

Shayua leaned back in her chair and took a long drink from her cup. Her eyes never left his. Nolan began to shift uncomfortably in his seat under that stare. When the bounty hunter slammed her cup down on the table, he nearly jumped out of his chair.

"Alright, Nolan Bintershad. Before Ezzy returns we need to come to an agreement. First, we must acknowledge that I know as little about your beliefs as you do about mine. We should not let our ignorance affect how we interact with each other and Ezzy."

"Agreed. I won't think of you as a brute and a killer, and you won't think of me as a frail know-it-all."

A small smile touched her lips. "Exactly. And to alleviate some of your fears, know that when given the option of capturing a bounty dead or alive, Avien'zia would rather her hunters take a prey alive. That is the idea I have pressed on Ezzy and will continue to promote. I want her to take this Ean fellow alive just as strongly as you do."

"That does make me feel better."

"Good, then the last thing I ask of you is to let her find her own way. If becoming a true devotee to Avien'zia is not what she is meant to do, it will be made obvious to us all. But do not try and hinder her from discovering her own path one way or another. Only two people can make that decision. Ezzy or Avien'zia herself."

"I can manage that, as long as you do not try to keep secrets from me." He raised a hand as she leaned forward, a scowl appearing on her face. "What I mean is that any decision or plan that involves her and our next course of action should be discussed as a group. Not decided between the two of you and then told to me after the fact."

"That is acceptable. Shall we make a pact on it then?"

Nolan hid his hands underneath the table. "I don't think blood needs to be involved to seal this particular deal."

This earned a great bellowing laugh from the woman.

"Not every deal involves the merging of blood. Again you show how little you know about my goddess and our practices."

"Oh. Well then." He felt his cheeks start to color. "A handshake?"

"Yes, a simple handshake will be fine."

———— ◆ ————

"Good," he said, extending his hand. "I wasn't sure that--"

He cut off as Shayua spit on her palm and extended it towards him. Although her face had taken on a serious look, her lip trembled as if holding back a smile. Shaking his head ruefully, he spit into his own hand and then grasped hers.

It was at just that moment that Ezzy walked up to them.

"Should I take this as a sign the two of you will stop going at each other's throats?"

"Yes," Nolan replied.

"Less than before at least." Shayua said at almost the same time.

"Good, because we have much to do. Let's order some food, rest our feet for a moment, and then it's time to work. The day is still young, and we have a Saniteal to find."

Chapter Nineteen

An Improper Welcome

"Alright, if you are both finished eating," Ezzy said, rising from her chair. "Let's get going."

Nolan tried to protest, but his mouth was full of a juicy piece of pig meat. Thankfully, Shayua spoke up.

"Slow down, girl. If this Saniteal is here, he won't suddenly disappear because we took too long to eat."

"He might..."

"Ezzy," Nolan said though a mouth full of pork. Holding up his index finger, he indicated for her to wait. After he swallowed, he continued. "Shayua's right. Let us enjoy our meal without feeling rushed. You did say I needed my rest after all."

"Glad all it took was a handshake for the two of you to gang up on me."

"When we both are speaking with wisdom," Shayua said in a lecturing tone, "it is not us 'ganging up' on you."

"I could just go out on my own if you two are going to be difficult--"

"Stop pouting," Shayua said, slapping the table. "It is a ploy by the weak willed to manipulate the even weaker willed. It will not work on us."

It had worked on Nolan. Quite a few times to be honest. Probably would have gotten him moving in this situation as well. His stomach thanked the bounty hunter as he grabbed another slice of pork. Shayua was handling this well, no need for him to speak up.

"Fine, fine." Ezzy returned to her seat. She grabbed a slice of meat off of Nolan's plate and bit off a piece. "I suppose a few more moments wouldn't be too painful."

"Glad you can act like an adult."

Although Shayua had gotten what she wanted, the woman frowned at something behind both Nolan and Ezzy. She was certainly strange. Didn't matter to Nolan though. He ate another slice of meat and washed it down with some ale before speaking.

"So, who is this contact we're going to see?"

"The local blacksmith." Ezzy leaned in and lowered her voice. "The woman's name is Syla, and she has been a loyal employee of my family for years. My father bought her loyalty a long time ago. He provided all of the funds for her to set up her shop here and used the smithy to keep track of the Janpair family up until he died."

"Ezzy," Nolan said, leaning forward as well, "you do realize that the smithy hasn't been paid by your family in quite some time. It's doubtful that she would remain loyal after her meal ticket has stopped."

"Not everything is about money, Nolan. Anyway, do you know how hard it is to set up a new show when the Janpair family owns the town? Even without a seasonal payment, considering everything my father did to help her get started, she owes him--owes me--her undying gratitude."

"Most things in this world are about money, Ezzy. People are quick to abandon their past loyalties when it makes their present a little easier and their future look more profitable."

"You're just a cynic. It's not like I'm asking her to kidnap the man or break into the Janpair home. All I'm going to do is ask her if she knows anything about our Saniteal and if this Iacane fellow is still in town."

"Still, maybe it would be best if we ask a few other sources. I noticed there is a healer set up in town. Surely a Saniteal would seek him or her out."

"Oh really? Would you seek out a maker of puppets in every village you visit?"

"Of course not. To compare what I do to a simple toy maker...oh, I see "

"Exactly. Any Saniteal I've met has looked down on healers and their use of plants and potions to cure injury and disease instead of magic. You certainly won't find him--"

"Quiet," Shayua hissed.

"What?" Ezzy pulled back. "What's the matter?"

"There is a great deal more people here at the inn than when we came in."

"So?" Ezzy turned and surveyed the room. "All I see are men in work clothes, probably taking a break from their jobs to get a quick drink and a meal."

"Then why are so many carrying weapons?"

Nolan swung around. Sure enough, over a dozen new men were now spread about the various tables, and each one had a weapon clearly displayed just as Shayua said. Most wore a short sword or long knife at their waist while a few had brazenly placed their weapons on the tables in front of them. Each one was making an effort NOT to look in their direction. All of the patrons that had been there when they first arrived were gone as well.

"Ezzy, I think Shayua is right. Something here isn't right..."

Just then the doors swung open and the most bizarrely dressed man walked in. He wore a red and orange striped coat that looked as if the same person that had painted the inn used the same orange to put stripes on a red coat. His pants were grey in color and hung loosely from his legs as if they were two sizes too big for him. They swirled about as he walked, almost like a dress. Greasy black hair, parted in the middle, framed his face. He strode into the room wearing a broad grin as he moved straight towards their table.

"Good evening, wonderful guests! Welcome to Shade." His voice was high pitched and contained an accent that Nolan couldn't place.

"It's barely midday, sir," one of the seated men said.

Not breaking his stride, the garishly dressed man backhanded the man who spoke as he walked by him.

"Quiet, fool. It's rude to correct your betters. Now, where was I? Ah yes! Welcoming our new guests!"

He stopped a few paces from their table and gave a mixture of a bow and a curtsy at the same time. When he rose again, he looked at each of them in turn, his eyes wide and not focused. When his attention landed on Ezzy, his smile somehow grew.

"Lady Ciantar! Quite the pleasure to have you in our quaint little village. Allow me to introduce myself. My name is Bavian Toll. I am the Janpair family's first man and your welcome party rolled into one. My employers have sent me down here to greet you and invite you back to the family estate for some pleasantries."

"A pleasant offer--" Nolan began, but the strange man cut him off, grabbing his hand and shaking it vigorously.

"And you must be Nolan Bintershad, the famous Thaljori! Well, not as famous as the one who bonded that behemoth in Rensen, huh? But still well-known amongst the elite of the realm. I'm sure now that the Ciantar family can no longer pay for your services, you are looking for permanent employment? I have no doubt that the Janpair family would be happy to put you on the payroll. Unless of course you have already started to lose your mind?"

"Now wait a minute..." Ezzy began but the man just kept on talking.

"And who is this tall, crimson drink of water?" He bowed again as he directed his question to Shayua. "Your skin tone is simply breathtaking. Is it paint or have you simply spent too much time out in the sun? Or maybe it's something altogether different. Ohhh, please tell me you've been touched by the Abyss. Those silly Seekers always kill people corrupted by the Abyss before anyone gets the chance to see them. So probably not that. Are you the bastard child of some gross mixing of the races?"

With a growl, Shayua quickly stood up, her chair crashing into the wall as she kicked it behind her in the process. Every single man in the room was on his feet in an instant, weapons in hand.

Bavian let out a laugh and Nolan began to wonder about the man's sanity. If Shayua towered over him wearing the same look of pure rage, Nolan would already be out the door or at the very least standing behind all of those other men and their weapons. Even knowing she was more or less on his side, Nolan wanted to take a few steps back from the woman. Bavian, on the other hand, looked like he didn't have a care in the world, and it reflected in his voice.

"No need to worry, old chaps. Our red giantess here won't be a problem, although it does look like she can't take a joke. Unless of course something I said was the truth? Too much sun? Are you a mutt?"

"I'll show you a mutt..."

Shayua was around the table before either Nolan or Ezzy could make a move to stop her. She threw a punch meant to floor the man, letting out a grunt as she swung. The man stepped out of the way with ease, barely shifting his body. With a growl, Shayua sent a few more punches his way, but the man continued to dodge them without showing any sign of distress. When Shayua took a moment to pause, the man applauded her, that same stupid grin painting his face.

"My, my," he said, not the least bit out of breath. "You are an aggressive...well I'm not sure what you are. I can see the human parts, of course, but what else makes up such an interesting girl?"

Shayua ignored his words and took up a more controlled fighting stance. Nolan watched her and kept an eye on the rest of the room at the same time. The other men scattered around the room had put their weapons away, although they remained standing. Most also wore a smile or smirk that made Nolan even more uneasy. What did they know?

"Oh, I've got it!" Bavian continued. "I can't believe I didn't think of it before. The strange skin color, the mindless aggression, and of course the two little tusks poking out of your mouth to say hello. You must be part Shadaer Umdaer! Fascinating! I do hope it was your mother that was Shadaer, as I can't see how a human female could have survived a night with one of those beasts--oooof"

Shayua landed a kick directly to the man's chest. The force of it, besides knocking the wind from him, sent the man rolling backwards in a blur of red, orange, and grey. He knocked over tables and chairs in his wake, eventually coming to rest a good fifteen or so paces from where he had been standing. Bavian laid there on his back for a few moments, barely moving. Nolan actually felt bad for the man. Clearly he wasn't in his right mind.

And then Bavian broke out in laughter.

Nolan watched in amazement as the man climbed to his feet. How could he still be moving? Nolan had seen the extent of the woman's more-than-human strength. A blow like that would have shattered bones if it had hit Nolan. Yet this man was not only getting right back to his feet, he was laughing about it! Bavian brushed himself off and continued to laugh with that high-pitched sound. Glancing at Shayua, Nolan saw she looked just as shocked as he felt. The anger seemed to drain from her face as she watched the man.

"What power!" Bavian said, not sounding the least bit in pain. "That is certainly from your Shadaer side. Fast too, to have actually hit me. My reflexes are better than any other human I know, but you got the drop on me with that one. You are truly a fascinating woman."

As the man began walking back towards them, Nolan noticed a glint of light reflect off of something on the back of the man's hands. His first thought was that Bavian had pulled out a blade, but looking closer it appeared that the man wore an array of iron rings on each of his fingers. They looked strange, though, almost as if they were all attached to each other...

"Now," Bavian continued, "my pretty crimson rose. Let's see if you've also inherited the famous Shadaer toughness."

Still wearing the same insane grin, the man struck, delivering a punch to Shayua's stomach. Bavian moved so fast that Shayua didn't even make a move to defend herself. She doubled over, gripping at her stomach, before dropping to her knees. And that's when the man unleashed another blow to the side of her head.

Shayua crumpled forward, her arms and legs limp. She smacked into the ground and remained still other than the intake of breath.

Ezzy was on her feet, one of the knives used to cut their food in her hand. Nolan struggled to rise as well. Before either of them was up, Bavian was kneeling near the fallen bounty hunter. He had a knife to her throat.

"Now, now. Let's not do anything foolish." He pointed his free hand towards Ezzy. "And you should certainly leave your Vilathos outside. Can't have it coming in and making a mess like you've done in countless other places. The inn's owner is a second cousin to the Janpair family. Or maybe it's a third cousin. No, strike that, they aren't related at all, but the inn keeper's wife makes an excellent apple pie that Mrs. Janpair loves... wait, what was I talking about?"

"What do you want?" Ezzy's monotone voice barely hid the anger behind it. Nolan only noticed it because he knew her so well.

"Oh yes. Shane and Leya Janpair, heads of the Janpair Hawkpurse family, would like to invite you to their mansion for drinks, dinner, and conversation."

"And if we are not feeling very social?"

"Then I'm to inform you that the invitation was an attempt to show some respect, despite the fact that your family has fallen into obscurity. If you want to insult them by refusing, my men and I have permission to 'escort' you up to the house. If it comes to that, the condition you arrive in is of no concern of theirs. Either way, you're going to dinner."

"Ok," Nolan jumped in before Ezzy's anger came bubbling out and got them into more trouble. "Just don't hurt Shayua, and as soon as we can wake her, we will all go with you."

Grabbing Shayua by the hair, Bavian lifted her up high enough so that they were face to face. The poor woman was still out cold, despite being lifted in such a painful fashion.

"This one wasn't given an invitation. I think it would be better if she stayed here and got some rest. I'll leave a few men to make sure she is comfortable. Of course, if your Vilathos was to even take a step from its current position, my men will make sure she never wakes up. Am I clear?"

"Perfectly," Ezzy replied through clenched teeth.

"I'll have them kill her. You did get that right?"

"Yes."

"Slit her throat and leave her for the buzzards."

"Enough! I get it. Let's go already."

"Excellent!"

Bavian released his grip and Shayua dropped, her head bouncing off the floor. He stepped out of the way as Ezzy rushed to her side. She turned the crimson woman over and checked to make sure she was breathing. Cradling Shayua's head, she shot a look at Bavian that made even Nolan flinch. The colorfully dressed man just smiled that insane smile back at her and shrugged his shoulders.

"Come, come. Let's be off. All this excitement has made me terribly hungry."

Not bothering to see if they followed, Bavian spun on his heels and walked away. Three of his men walked over to pick Shayua up.

"I swear," Ezzy growled, "if you are anything but gentle with her, I will make it my life's goal to make sure each of you is left alone in a locked room with her when she wakes. Do I make myself clear?"

The men paused for a moment as her words sunk in, then each man grabbed one of Shayua's muscular arms and lifted her up. It took them a bit of time to get the woman leaning back in a chair, especially since the other men kept their distance. All the while Ezzy watched them, the knife from the table back in her hand. Once the woman was situated, Ezzy turned her attention to Nolan.

"Let's get this over with."

"Agreed." Nolan replied.

"Don't forget what I said..." Ezzy took the time to look at each man remaining in the inn before nodding to Nolan.

Leaving the unconscious Shayua behind, Ezzy and Nolan left to meet the Janpairs.

Chapter Twenty

A Glimpse of an Old Life

"You're going to have a splendid time," Bavian said over his shoulder as they walked further into town. "The Janpair family spares no expense when it comes to spoiling their guests. Of course, that comes easy when you have such a vast amount of wealth. You know what that's like, Esmerelda, yes? Or I suppose you *did* know what that was like. Must be strange to go from having everything to living in a shack with the rest of the poor wretches in Lurthalan. Is it strange?"

"How about you keep your mouth shut." It was all Ezzy could do not to lunge at the man. Which was good, since if Bavian could put Shayua down so easily, Ezzy wouldn't stand much of a chance. Instead she was forced to try and stare a hole of hatred through his ugly striped coat. And listen to him babble on.

"I am many things, Ms. Ciantar, but quiet is not one of them. If you ask my employers, I'm flamboyant, blunt, loyal, and possibly psychotic. Not sure what the first word means, but I believe the other words are compliments. Of course, they pay so well, they could call me whatever they wanted and I wouldn't mind. Plus, they let me entertain myself. It's doubtful I could have as much fun in Lurthalan or one of the smaller villages as I do here. People would complain too much. Do you like it here? I certainly do. The wall sings at night you know. Like a lullaby just for the villagers here."

He gestured to the Unyielding Wall towering over the village. Made of blocks larger than any house in Shade, it stretched high into the sky, lost in the clouds high above them. From this close, it almost felt like it was leaning towards them, on the verge of toppling over. Ezzy hadn't realized it when they first got to the village, but now it felt oppressive. She had to stop looking at it. As much as it pained her, Ezzy returned her attention to Bavian.

"I've heard that living this close to the wall changes people. Messes with their head. Is that why you wear such ugly clothing?"

"You don't like?" Bavian spun about, arms wide, while still moving forward. He didn't stumble in the slightest. "I had a famous tailor create it for me. Have you heard about the genius tailor of Shade?"

"No, I can't say I have."

"Sure you have. His name is Bavian Toll!"

The man let out a laugh and spun a few more times.

"Sorry, never heard of you."

Letting out a sigh, Bavian stopped spinning.

"Of course not. That's the problem with never being allowed out of the village. No one gets to see my creativity except for the few dozen families that live here."

"Such a shame you can't be out offending the eyes of more people," Nolan said. He had been quiet since they had left the inn. Ezzy had almost forgotten he was there.

"It is! So glad you understand my plight, Master Thaljori. Anyway, enough about me. Is this your first time here? I should be giving you the tour!"

"I can look around fine without your running commentary," Ezzy said. To her surprise, Bavian grew quiet, allowing her to take in her surroundings.

Besides the looming Wall, Shade looked no different from any other village or town in Ven Khalida. The road they followed circled around an open patch of grass. She spotted a smith's shop, healer's shop, and a general store that lined the circle. A few side streets branched off and seemed to lead towards more homes. Bavian took them left off the circle and down another street. They passed a few homes on either side and then cut down a side street that climbed a low hill. It led to a walled-in home with a massive and ornate metal gate.

"Welcome to the Janpair estate," Bavian said with open arms. "You won't find a more comfortable home."

As Bavian lead them through the open gates, Ezzy felt a twinge of sadness. Although not exactly the same, the homestead held many characteristics similar to her former home. They walked onto an open courtyard, with a fountain and intricately painted tiles that made a pathway to the main house. To her left sat a small building and a stable, with a garden sitting behind it in the northwest corner. The main house itself took up a good portion of the right side, a three-story brick building with a multitude of windows and a red tiled roof. Small potted plants hung from each window and a small patio extended out from the second floor. Despite what Ezzy might think about their choice of employees, the Janpairs had a beautiful home.

Bavian lead them straight to the front door and pulled on a rope hanging from the wall. A loud gong sounded once before the front door opened. Their guide stepped to the side, extending a hand for them to enter. Ezzy pushed past the man and stepped into the home. She just wanted to get this over with and return to check on Shay.

The extravagance of the inside matched its outside appearance. The main entranceway was a large, open room with a double staircase in the middle that curved upstairs. A chandelier with crystals that made the room sparkle hung from the center of the ceiling. Various works of art hung on the walls and sat atop pedestals around the room. Ezzy didn't know a single thing about art or who created it. To her it was all just the work of those that couldn't handle having a real job. She would never understand why people would pay so much more just for the name behind it.

What she did find interesting, however, was the man that opened the door for them. Or the woman. Ezzy could never tell when it came to the Taruun race.

Whatever it was, the Taruun towered over them. Ezzy's eyes were only as high as the man's waist, which was thinner than hers. That didn't tell her much, though. All Taruuns were thin and gangly, which made their incredible strength all the more surprising. Tilting her head back to get a look at its head, she found a face like so many others she had seen before. Pale, almost marble-colored skin seemed chiseled from stone, with harsh lines and edges where on a human you would find gentle curves. His jet black eyes sat deep in that face, almost hidden in shadow. What Ezzy found most interesting was that he/she was dressed in a normal servant's white vest and black coat and pants that clung to his body. It was a sharp contrast to a Taruun's usual attire of baggy, bland colored clothes.

"Hello, Butler," Bavian said as he patted the Taruun on the arm. "So kind of you to let us in. Be a good chap and let our masters know we are here."

Without a word, Butler closed the door and ascended the stairs. As the towering--Ezzy assumed now it was a man--shuffled up the steps, Bavian returned his attention to her and Nolan.

"A pleasant enough fellow. Not much for conversation, but he knows a few dozen human words at least."

As much as Ezzy had no desire to talk to the man, her curiosity won her over.

"The Janpairs have a Taruun for a servant? From what I've been taught, the Taruun have never been known to take servant positions. As a matter of fact, I've never heard of one working on anything that didn't involve a tree. How did the Janpairs even get one to leave the forest for a long period of time?"

"Simple. They bought him."

"What?" It took Ezzy a little bit to realize the man was being serious. "The temples outlawed slavery decades ago. He can't be a slave."

"And yet he is! Been one for years. They bought him as a child, or so I've been told."

"That's horrible! How do they get away with keeping the Taruun against his will?"

"Is that a real question? They are a Hawkpurse family. They do as they please, especially in a village they control. Grow up, little girl. You of all people should know what kind of power the Hawkpurse families wield."

"My family never--"

"Shhh." Bavian stuck a finger out as if to touch Ezzy's lips. When she made a move to bite him, the man retracted his finger. "You can talk all about your family to my employers. Ah, and it seems that they are ready to receive you."

Butler was standing at the top of the stairs and waving them up. Bavian began to move, forcing Ezzy and Nolan to follow or be left standing in the entrance hall. Climbing the stairs, they came to a landing that split to the left and right, with a large set of double doors in front of them. The doors were made of a dark wood, with intricate designs depicting the god, Drenks, drinking and carrying on. The only thing Ezzy had been happy about when her family home burned down was that all of the effigies and pictures of Drenks had been reduced to ash. She hoped that burnt and broken statues still sat in the rubble of her home.

When they had all reached the top of the stairs, Butler opened the doors and led them through.

The room they entered was even more extravagant than the entranceway. Black banners with silver trim hung everywhere, a green snake coiled around a bag of money adorning every one. Among the banners, portraits of men and women took up the rest of the wall space. Golden candelabras lit up the room. Swampsilk rugs of dark reds and light blues adorned the dark hardwood floor, the material sparkling from all of the candle light. In the middle of the room sat a long table, covered by a dark crimson tablecloth. Plates of every type of food imaginable sat spread out along the top. Roasted pigs, a huge slab of beef, fruit, vegetables, various bowls of soups, cakes, and other deserts, and a dozen or so other foods that Ezzy couldn't even think of their names. Even though she had just had something to eat at the inn, the sight and smell of all of that food made her stomach rumble. Seated at the head of the table were their hosts, Shane and Leya Janpair.

Ezzy had only seen the pair once before, and that had been when she was still playing with dolls. From what she remembered and how they looked now, the years had been kind to Shane and Leya. Shane sat on the left, a man not late in his years, but with a touch of grey spotting his short black hair. Green eyes examined her behind a long pointed nose. He wore a black silk shirt, the sleeves cuffed at his elbows, and a gold medallion hung around his neck. His body was rigid as he sat straight up in his chair, as if he were trying very hard to look formal.

Leya had made quite an impression on Ezzy during their one encounter, and the woman was as beautiful as Ezzy remembered her. Her golden hair sat up in a bun, the sparkle of meticulously placed jewels reflecting the candle light. Her petite nose and mouth accentuated her slightly larger dark blue eyes. She wore an elegant blue dress covered in tiny jewels that hugged her body in all the right places. Ezzy wasn't one to get jealous of the looks of other women, but Leya certainly tested her self-confidence. Many of her father's servants had also noticed the woman's stunning looks and had talked about her for days after the Janpairs had visited.

"Ah, our honored guests!" Shane said, rising to his feet. "So happy that you could accept our invitation. It is so rare that we get visitors of your caliber to our quaint little village, Ms. Ciantar. As you can see, we spared no expense to make this quite the enjoyable meal. So little is known about you or your tastes that I had my cooks make as wide a variety as possible. Come, sit. Let us talk of the finer things."

He paused for a moment, his gaze wandering off to the side.

"Yes, I know," he said as if to thin air. "I'll ask her later. Now isn't the time."

His attention snapped back to Ezzy and Nolan and he waved at them to sit. They moved to opposite sides of the table, with Ezzy using the time to try and figure out what Shane had meant. Bavian, meanwhile, walked over to the Janpair family and stood a few paces behind them. Once they were all seated, Leya picked up her glass and raised it.

"To the Janpair and Ciantar families. May our two great families find fortune and favor in the eyes of the gods."

Ezzy couldn't tell if the woman was being sincere or sarcastic. Certainly they had heard of her family's downfall. Was she trying to rub that fact in her face or just being polite? Not quite sure what to make of the toast, Ezzy's years of training in manners kicked in and she raised her glass as well, giving her host a nod of thanks. Nolan might think she was brash and quick to anger, but she knew how to handle herself in social situations such as these. Until Shane took a moment to pour a little of what was in his glass onto the floor. That was certainly not a custom she was familiar with. The day was getting more confusing with every moment.

When the silence of the moment dragged on and Ezzy realized the Janpairs were staring at her, the thought occurred to her that they might be expecting her to say something.

"I...want to thank you for your gracious invitation and the meal you have prepared for Nolan and myself. This array of food is as extravagant as your home."

That sounded proper.

"So nice of you to notice," Shane said. "We have a quaint home out here so far away from Lurthalan, but we try to have it live up to the expectations placed on us as Hawkpurses. What? No, later. I'll ask later."

Again, Shane spoke to his side, although no one was there. Ezzy glanced at Nolan, who shrugged, and then looked at her other host. Leya was smiling, but it held no warmth. Her gaze was locked on Ezzy, looking at her like Shayua looked at a rabbit she had just pulled from a snare. Ezzy shifted uncomfortably in her seat.

"Anyway, before I was interrupted," Shane continued, frowning off to his side, "it's so rare we get to show off our home to anyone. The other Hawkpurse families don't visit, and no one in the village warrants an audience to dine with us. It's nice to be able to sit and enjoy a meal with such well-respected members of the realm."

Well-respected? Everyone in Lurthalan knew her family now lived in the slums and treated her family as such. The man must be trying to insult her in a backhanded sort of way. Well, under normal circumstances that might be how the high and mighty spoke to each other, but no matter how much of a show Shane and Leya were putting on, Ezzy and Nolan had been forced here. Ezzy had had enough of being proper.

"Why are we really here?" Nolan gave a loud cough, but Ezzy ignored him. "You send your man to bring us here by force if needs be, flaunt your wealth and Taruun slave, and then continue to offer me backhanded compliments when you know how far my family has fallen. If you want a 'pleasant meal,' then I want some answers."

Shane stared at her, confusion painting his face. Leya, on the other hand, let out a laugh before speaking.

"I was told you were a straight forward woman, and I'm happy that the reports weren't exaggerated. I would have been disappointed if this meal had been a boring display of all of us trying to appear like we were best of friends while cutting into each other with our words. A meal with all of us tossing aside all of the formalities will be much more enjoyable. At least for me."

"You haven't answered my question."

"Fair enough, Esmerelda. Since you want to toss decorum and civility aside, I will give you a straight answer to your question. I had you brought here like a common prisoner for the simple fact that I wanted to meet you in person before I decided whether or not to have Bavian take you outside and kill you."

Chapter Twenty-One

DINNER CONVERSATIONS

"Well," Ezzy replied, "that certainly is not what I expected to hear."

"Of course not," Shane said with a laugh. "Whoever expects to be told they might be killed? Other than those put to death ...and maybe soldiers or guards... I suppose...."

Leya put a gentle hand on her husband's shoulder, which quieted him as soon as he felt her touch. Their eyes met, and some warmth appeared in the woman's face. When she returned her gaze to Ezzy, however, that warmth was gone.

"You are a riddle. With as much as I know about the Hawkpurse families, which spans both before and after the Plague, I have never seen any mention of a family losing its status as a Hawkpurse. And for the Ciantar family to be the first to fall? When your family dissolved, I assumed the Ciantar name would disappear into obscurity. I believed that Drenks himself would have wiped your family from the land. This does not seem to be the case."

"What can I say, we Ciantar are hardy people."

"Something I already knew. To be given the duty of trading with those in the Deadlands speaks to your family's survivability. Even if that is where your father died."

Ezzy moved her hands underneath the table and clenched them into fists. "My father died because of the actions of one man. He turned those in the north against my father and his caravan."

"And now the one village in the Deadlands that traded with our realm has been reduced to ash. By some powerful creature, if you are to believe the reports. Is your mystery man responsible for this as well?"

"All I know for certain is the name of the man behind my father's death--Ean Sangrave--and I'm going to bring him in to face the justice of the temples."

"If you leave here alive."

"Yes."

"Interesting..."

"If I may say something..." Nolan tried to join the conversation but Leya's raised hand silenced him.

"You may not. Either Esmerelda will leave and I assume you with her, or she will be killed and you will be unemployed. At which point we will offer you the chance to work for us. Until then, you may sit, enjoy the food and drink, but otherwise you will remain silent unless asked a question. Don't try to interject your opinion again. Understood?"

Nolan's face went pale. Ezzy's immediate impulse was to defend her friend, but for once she decided to take Nolan's advice and keep her temper in check. A silence hung over the room for a moment, then Shane broke it with a giggle.

"Yes, yes, I'll ask her." Again he spoke to the air at his side. "No need to dance around with formalities now."

He returned his attention to Ezzy although his eyes did not seem to focus. What was wrong with the man?

"Esmerelda. What is it like being bonded to a Vilathos? I would imagine it's like having something make a home in your mind."

"Well... yes, it is similar to that." Not sure how else to respond, Ezzy took the opportunity to take a sip from the cup in front of her. It contained a deliciously spiced wine that tingled as it touched her tongue. Was the man just making conversation, or did ulterior motives prompt the question? Shane seemed disinterested in the conversation she was having with Leya. He also seemed to be a little off. Not crazy per say, but certainly eccentric. His wife wasn't interrupting him though, so maybe he was prying for information? Ezzy struggled to figure out what was going on, which gave Shane the opportunity to speak.

"That is so very strange. I can't even begin to imagine what that must be like." Again he turned to speak to his side. "What? Oh no, it's not the same. Plus, the Thaljori said I had too many holes in my mind to bond..."

"Husband," Leya interrupted, "we are getting off topic. I'm sure the topic of Vilathos can be discussed later."

"As you wish, my love. Dopa had just wanted me to ask--"

"Perhaps you should allow me to do the talking, while you and Dopa listen and try to figure out if our guest is lying."

Glancing around the room, Ezzy tried her best to find this Dopa fellow hiding nearby but found no one. She even tried looking underneath the table but didn't find even a hint of another person in the room. Letting her curiosity win out, she decided to just ask.

"Who is Dopa?"

"No one you need to concern--"

"Dopa is my most trusted advisor," Shane cut his wife off, leaning forward with an excited expression. "A magical creature that appeared from out of The Wall. He is wise and insightful, and the best part is that he is invisible!"

Bavian laughed. When Leya slowly turned to stare at the man, he instantly stopped laughing, looking as if he was about to wet himself. Ezzy glanced uneasily back to the beautiful Leya. What was it about her that made a psychopath like Bavian so afraid? It was as if everyone here was infected with madness.

"Shane, my love," Leya turned her attention back to her husband. "Remember, you were wanting to keep your advisor's presence a secret. Other people wouldn't approve of him. If they knew, you would be pressured to send him away. And we can't have that now, can we?"

The man sat back and began to pout. "I only told Esmerelda, and she is probably going to die soon. Where is the harm in that?"

"I...I mean, we... have yet to decide Esmerelda's fate. It's rude of you to say otherwise."

Shane rolled his eyes and then nodded. Ezzy watched as that warmth returned to Leya's face and she patted her husband's hand. The woman really did love him, despite his clear mental issues. Maybe she was crazy too. Glancing around, Ezzy tried to find something that might help her and Nolan escape. A cough from Leya brought her attention back to her host.

"As I was saying, I have some questions to ask you. The first one being, why are you here?"

"Because Bavian said you'd have us killed if we didn't come."

"Ah, that Bavian. He does enjoy his jokes. What I mean is, do I have your assurance that you're not here seeking your justice on anyone else besides this Ean fellow? And for that matter, why do you think he is here in Shade?"

"By 'anyone else,'" Ezzy stated, "you mean the Hawkpurses for their ill-treatment of my family after my father's death?"

Leya nodded.

"If I wanted revenge on everyone that may have been against my family, I'd need an army of Vilathos. But rest assured, all I care about, at the moment, is finding Ean."

"And you believe he is here?"

"No, but I think a man that might know where to find him is somewhere in your village."

"So you are not here to seek revenge on my family? For what happened to your family's empire and the destruction of your home?"

That caught Ezzy off-guard.

"Were you responsible for the destruction of our home?"

"No, but you know how the Hawkpurses plot and deceive. I had thought maybe one of the other houses had pointed you in our direction."

"The other houses won't even sell my family a scrap of bread. We have had to survive by buying from the more expensive free traders in Lurthalan. As far as I know, the other families would rather just see mine disappear into nothingness. Yours is the first to even acknowledge that I'm alive."

"I see..." Leya looked less than convinced.

"My only goal," Ezzy continued, "at the moment, is to find the man that caused my father's death. After he is brought to justice, then I'll focus on who kicked the legs out from under my already crippled family. If you are lying and were a part of that, then you have some time to make amends before I come after you."

"Bravo, girl!" Shane began to clap then noticed no one else was joining in and stopped.

"Such spirit," Leya said once her husband had grown quiet. "It's refreshing to see a woman take charge of her family's affairs. A pity your house has been brought so low."

"I'm tired of hearing--"

"Brought low, but not wiped out. You might raise your family out of the ashes one day, become a Hawkpurse again. Maybe you can even undo whatever your family did that made Drenks abandon you and return to the Hawkpurse ranks."

"Drenks has abandoned my family, so I've abandoned him. But make no mistake about it, I *will* bring my family's name back out of the mire."

"Fewer Hawkpurses around means a bigger slice of the trading pie for the rest of us. Still, I feel an affinity towards you. After all, somewhere down the line, we are kin. I would hate to see your family's name completely disappear."

"As would I."

"Well then, you have my...our family's support. Not with money or manpower, but you can see us as not your enemy, at least. Can we think of you in the same manner?"

"Was your family responsible for the destruction of my home?"

"No."

"Then I don't consider you my enemy."

"Excellent!" Shane interjected. "Then we can finally eat!"

He grabbed the closest serving tray and began shoveling the food onto his plate.

"So glad we don't have to kill you. Now we can talk of more pleasant things."

Ezzy let herself smile. As crazy as the man was, he was a jovial fellow. And Nolan certainly hadn't wasted any time. He had a mouthful of food and was cutting into a piece of meat. He paused for a moment when Ezzy's eyes met his, then shrugged and kept eating. Not wanting to appear rude, Ezzy picked up a thick cob of corn and took a bite. The buttery kernels overwhelmed her tastebuds with their sweetness.

"Now that we've removed some of the tension," Leya said. "Why don't you tell us who you're looking for that is supposed to point you in the direction of this Ean fellow?"

"Mmmph...a Saniteal..." Ezzy said, trying to talk and chew at the same time. "His name is Iacane."

"I've heard of him,' Shane said. "Been in the village for almost a whole season."

"Do you know where?"

"No. I haven't needed his services."

"What my husband doesn't know," Leya said, "is that the Saniteal has gone missing recently. The home where he was staying reported that he hadn't returned one night, but his things are still there."

"Have you tried to find him?"

"No, it didn't seem important."

"A missing person in your village didn't seem important?"

"Why would--"

A loud boom interrupted her. Followed by another. The third shook the table and was followed by the sound of splintering wood. Leya made a motion with her hand and Bavian was on his way to the doors. Just as he reached them, they burst open, showering splinters everywhere. Bavian rolled backwards and was back on his feet in an instant. Everyone else was out of their chairs.

Shayua came storming through the entryway, a snarl on her lips.

"Shay, it's alright," Ezzy said, moving towards the woman. "This is just a bit of a misunderstanding. They handled us a little roughly but--"

The force of the larger woman backhanding Ezzy across the chest lifted her off her feet and tossed her to the side. She landed hard, her vision swimming as she tried to fight off unconsciousness. Struggling to rise, she watched as Shayua stalked towards Bavian.

"Want another lesson?" Bavian said.

He stood his ground, not seeming bothered by the towering woman. Shayua didn't respond. She walked right up to the man and started swinging. Bavian dodged the blows almost as easily as he had earlier in the day, but something was different with Shayua's attacks. They seemed more ferocious, more wild. There was no finesse as she swung again and again at the man.

"Enough fun," Bavian panted. "Time to put you down."

Ducking under a punch, he landed four quick blows to the woman's stomach. He might as well have been flicking her from what little reaction Shayua gave to the blows. She just continued swinging at the man.

It was then that Ezzy noticed the woman's eyes. The pupils and white of her eyes were gone, replaced with a dark blue color.

"Something's wrong with her! Look at her eyes!"

"Difficult to do," Bavian said as he dodged another blow, "while she is trying to kill me."

"Get her outside!"

Bavian ducked under another punch and sprinted for the door. Shayua was right on his heels. Once outside the room, he paused in front of the rail overlooking the entranceway. As Shayua charged at him, he leapt out of the way at the last moment. The bounty hunter didn't slow as she crashed through the railing and dropped from sight.

"I said get her outside," Ezzy screamed, running up to Bavian and what was left of the railing. "Not kill her."

"A minor fall would kill that beast? I was hoping I would get lucky and she would knock herself out." He pointed down to where Shayua was getting to her feet. "I'm never lucky."

"Just get her outside before she brings the house down around us," Leya said from the shattered doorway.

"Fine, fine."

Shayua began stomping up the left staircase, her eyes still dark blue. There was a bit of froth on her lips as well. Her feet pounded on the stairs, the railing shaking with each step. When she was almost to the top, Bavian took off down the right staircase.

"I wouldn't stand in her way!" he called over his shoulder.

Glancing at Shayua and seeing nothing but pure rage in her snarling lips and glaring eyes, she decided the man was right. Ezzy raced down the stairs after him. Shay let out a primal scream behind them. Not wanting to be caught by someone who could make such a terrifying noise, Ezzy pushed herself even harder, taking the stairs three at a time. On the ground floor, she found the front door in the same condition as the one leading to the dining room. Butler was sitting nearby, a small gash on his head marring his porcelain skin. Bavian was already out the door and Ezzy sprinted right behind him.

"Ok, we're outside," Bavian panted. "Now what?"

"Now we get help."

Just as Shayua stormed out of the building, Paz lumbered through the gate.

"Oh, this should be interesting."

Ezzy sent Paz charging towards her mentor. His long strides put him there in just a few steps, and he stood with outstretched arms waiting for the bounty hunter. Now slowing down, Shayua let out a roar and leapt on the Vilathos. She landed on its chest and held on to its neck. Scrambling up its front, Shayua wrapped her legs around its metal head and began raining down blows. Even though Paz was made entirely of metal and was strengthened by the magic that gave it the semblance of life, Shayua's massive hands began making small dents in the dome of Paz's head.

"Hey! Don't break him!"

Shayua continued to pound away, seemingly oblivious to anyone else around her. With a thought, Ezzy had Paz wrap both of its hands around the bounty hunter, pinning her arms to her sides. She struggled against him, but even her incredible strength couldn't break free from its iron grip. Finally contained, Ezzy let out a sigh of relief. She had Paz walk her over, but not close enough that Shayua could lash out and catch her with a kick.

"Shayua, what's wrong with you?"

Nothing. A snarl and glare was the only response she received.

"I've never seen anything like that," Bavian said as he reached her side. "I've beaten up or killed a fair number of people in my lifetime, but I've never seen anyone take some of my best punches with my knuckle dusters without even the slightest reaction."

"Do you think it's some kind of magic?"

"Could be, although I've never heard of anything like it. She seemed to have lost all...oh look."

Ezzy watched as the dark blue color drained from her eyes. Her head drooped and her body went limp in Paz's grip. After a moment, Shayua lifted her head and looked around. Her eyes were only partially opened and she seemed to struggle to get the words out when she spoke.

"What happened?"

"You tell me," Ezzy said. "You went a bit nutty. It was almost like you were possessed. What do you remember?"

"Not much. I remember being struck by this fool," she shot Bavian a glare that would have curdled milk, "and then waking up on the inn floor. I was so angry that such a little man had taken me down, I felt like I was going to burst. Then nothing. I have no idea how I got here or why your metal beast has me crushed between its hands."

"I would like to let you go, Shay, but how do I know you won't go crazy again?"

The bounty hunter shrugged as best as she could in the hands of the Vilathos.

"I don't know what to tell you. Nothing like that has ever happened to me before as far as I can remember. Do what you must."

Well, you're no help. But I can't keep you wrapped up forever.

With a thought, she had Paz set the crimson woman down. Free of its grasp, Shayua began to stretch and rub at her arms. She kept her eyes locked on Bavian.

"No hard feelings?" Bavian asked, spreading his arms wide. "I was just following orders and you did attack first."

"I do not hold grudges for being bested in combat, little man. I do remember when I've been insulted, however."

"Yes, yes. Understandable. Sometimes my mouth does get a bit out of control, especially when I encounter something as strange as you."

Shayua scowled at him.

"Unusual! Not strange! Unusual! See, there I go again saying the wrong words at the wrong time. A funny saying. Is there a right time to say the wrong words? That doesn't make much sense, does it? Of course, the right words at the right time would be wonderful, but never seems to happen for me. Maybe I should start again."

"Or maybe," Leya said as she strode out the shattered front door, "you should simply stop talking."

Chapter Twenty-Two

A Step in the Right Direction

"As you command," Bavian replied with a bow. "Forgive my wagging tongue; I am always the Janpair's faithful servant."

"Quite." Striding past the man, Leya walked up to Shayua. Although dwarfed by the bounty hunter, Leya stood in front of her with her nose high in the air, shoulders back, voice steady and dignified. "You have made a mess of my house and frightened my poor husband."

"Shayua doesn't remember what she did," Ezzy said, coming to her mentor's defense. "Something happened to her that made her lose control. She wasn't herself. I'm sure she regrets what happened."

Leya let out a laugh.

"After a few too many glasses of wine, I sometimes make decisions that I regret the next morning. That doesn't make it any less my fault. I have half a mind to have this woman locked up. The other half of my mind thinks I should have her flogged and then locked up."

"I assume you are Leya Janpair," Shayua said with downcast eyes. "I apologize for any destruction I have caused your home. Although I do not know why I acted the way I did, I do accept the responsibility for my actions and will submit to whatever punishment you feel is just."

"That quickly? You must either be a worshipper of Alistar or Avien'zia then. Only proper followers of one of those two would submit to judgment without a fight. Which is it?"

"Avien'zia."

"With your size and strength, it is obvious that you're a bounty hunter. Tell me one thing then. Why are you so far from your homeland?"

"I left Lurthalan to catch--"

"No, no. I wasn't asking why you left your current home. By 'homeland,' I meant where you were born."

"I was born in the city of Lurthalan." Shayua's voice was strained. "That is where I have lived all my life."

"Do you take me for a fool? You are clearly a Shadaer, although the human in you is quite clear in some of your features. I was unaware that the two races could produce offspring. Which of your parents was Shadaer? Your mother? Your father?"

"I did not know my father." A tinge of anger touched her voice for a moment before she got control of it.

"So your father was Shadaer. Interesting. And irrelevant. I was simply curious. Your lineage has nothing to do with your punishment."

"Good."

"Tough one, aren't you? Well, Shayua, as much as I should have you flogged, I won't. You seem to know little of your own people, so I assume you know nothing of the Rage that can overtake them. Your ignorance combined with the fact that Esmerelda and I have just recently come to a mutual understanding, has earned you some lenience. Pay me fifteen gold pieces for all of the repairs, and you may be on your way."

"I do not have that much money."

"I do," Ezzy said, reaching for her coin purse.

"Ezzy, I can't allow you to pay for me."

"Think of it as an advance for everything you plan on teaching me."

"I did not agree to teach you for money. It is the will of--"

"I know, I know. Avien'zia put us together. Think of it this way then. I am taking up your time and you can't catch bounties and make a living while you are accompanying me. Think of this as an investment and not a payment or gift."

"Ezzy, I don't know--"

"If it makes you feel any better, remember where this money comes from."

Shayua's face scrunched up in confusion for a moment. Then, as the realization hit her, she let out a deep, bellowing laugh.

"Yes, you are right. I feel much better about it, knowing it was the money of those Orange Hound scoundrels."

"Good, then it's settled. Here you are, Leya. We're all settled up."

"Excellent," Leya replied, taking the money. "Well then, if you will excuse me, I have much to do, first of which is to get my husband to come out from under our bed. You gave him quite a scare."

"Oh, dinner is over?" Nolan asked, the disappointment clear in his voice.

"Yes. You've brought enough excitement to my home for the day." Giving a slight nod to Ezzy, Leya turned and walked into the house, leaving the four of them standing in the courtyard. Bavian looked at each of them in turn, then shrugged.

"I suppose I should go too. I'll have plenty to do now to organize the cleanup. Good luck with... well, whatever it is you are doing." He leaned forward to whisper in Ezzy's ear. "I stopped listening as soon as you sat down at the table. Hawkpurse business can be dreadfully boring."

"We still have unfinished business," Shayua said as the man pulled back.

"Well," he replied, "when I'm a little less busy, we can finish our business. Have a little go. A fight I mean. Not the other physical thing, with the lack of clothes. Although a fight without clothes could be funny. Bits and pieces flopping about. Wait, did you want to fight without clothes?"

"No!"

"Well, you still have time. Give it some thought. Sleep on it."

Before Shayua could reply, Bavian gave a deep bow and then strode off. Leaving Ezzy, Shayua, and Nolan standing in the center of the property.

"Well, this has been an eventful day." Nolan said, glancing around.

"I'd say so," Ezzy replied. "But the day isn't over yet. We still have time to see the blacksmith and try to hunt down our missing Saniteal."

"Ezzy, surely we can go see him tomorrow."

"No, Nolan. I don't think so. If Iacane has gone missing, it could be because he is hurt or dying somewhere. Time is a factor."

"The man you are searching for has gone missing?" Shayua asked. "Then I agree, we should not waste time."

"You would agree," Nolan grunted. "No time to sit and catch our breath when there is a hunt to be had."

"Oh, Nolan, stop. You seemed relaxed as you were eating your second meal a few moments ago."

"I was eating because I was worried."

"You didn't look worried as you stuffed your face with--"

"Ok, ok. Let's go find your blacksmith."

Flashing him a smile, Ezzy headed towards the gate. Nolan and Shay followed with Paz taking up the rear. They walked back down to the main part of the village and returned to the circular road at the center of town. At this point in the day, more people were out and about, going about their business. Paz got his fair share of looks, but Shayua received the majority of stares from the villagers. The bounty hunter stared right back. Or glared would be the better word. At one point, Shayua looked like she was about to go after a group of young men that were pointing and laughing at her. Ezzy moved to her side before Shay's temper got the better of her.

"Is it always like this for you?"

"Not so much in Lurthalan. I keep mostly to the temple and the camps around it. The other worshippers have gotten used to me, I suppose."

"And Leya said you were part Shadaer?"

"I still do not wish to speak of this, Ezzy."

"Understood. I won't pry."

"Thank you."

They walked on in silence. Ezzy tried to glare at the gawkers as much as Shay to give her mentor some support. She also sent Paz back to the inn. After all, now that she was on good terms with the Janpair family, what other trouble could they get into here that Shayua couldn't get them out of?

Shayua. The woman was quite the mystery. Ezzy snuck a glance at the crimson bounty hunter. The more they traveled together, the more questions arose. She had mentioned growing up in the temple. What kind of a childhood could that have been? Probably the complete opposite of what Ezzy had experienced. In their own way, they both had had a strange childhood compared to most children in Lurthalan. Of course Shayua had been killing things while Ezzy had been learning about all of the extended family members in each of the other Hawkpurse families.

And to grow up like that around people that knew she was a half-breed? A Shadaer half-breed, no less. It certainly explained Shay's sensitivity about her past and her appearance. Ezzy didn't even know mixing the species was possible. Ezzy had only read about their savage neighbors to the south in books. A nomadic race, from what Ezzy remembered, that controlled a section of land just as large as Ven Khilada, bordered by the Skyfall Mountains to the west, the Unyielding Wall to the east, and the coast to the south. The Soushade Hawkpurses were the only ones allowed into their territory for trade, and from what Ezzy had heard, being allowed onto their land didn't guarantee safety. How had Shayua even been conceived, let alone make it out of the south to grow up in Lurthalan?

Ezzy hoped if they became close enough, and after she had finished hunting down those responsible for the downfall of her family, Shayua would tell her one day.

"Is this it?" Nolan was standing underneath a sign containing a sword embedded in an anvil.

"The sign looks about right. I didn't see any other signs that would indicate a blacksmith's shop."

"Let's go in and take a look then. I would love to be done with this for the day so I can go back to the inn and enjoy a nice, hot bath."

The inside of the shop was wide open in the middle, allowing Ezzy to see all around the store. Racks lined the walls, their contents ranging from simple blades and long swords to rakes, hammers, and an assortment of farming tools. A few shields and random pieces of armor were scattered about as well, but those were probably more for show than to actually sell. In the back of the room sat a small anvil and forge, a fire bellowing inside and belching smoke up the chimney behind it. The room was windowless, various candlesticks provided the light, and a solitary door in the far wall probably led to Syla's living quarters and the back of the building.

A woman was working the forge, a hammer in one hand and a short sword in the other. The sword blade glowed a fiery red and sparks flew off of it as she hammered the metal. Syla Trane. She didn't seem to notice as they entered, giving Ezzy a chance to get a good look at her. A short woman, Syla's braided auburn hair rested on her back. Her face was a rosy red from being so close to the fire, which accented chubby cheeks and a pronounced, pointed nose. Soot and dirt had turned her tan pants black. A sleeveless black apron showed off arms chiseled from years of hammering away on metal. She looked young, but Ezzy's mother had said that Syla had worked for their family for years. Years spent in this bizarre little village. Not wanting to startle the woman, Ezzy moved more into her line of sight and waved a hand to get her attention. Dark green eyes looked up from their work and regarded Ezzy with a blank expression for a moment before she put down her hammer and the blade.

"You're new..." Her tone was a mixture of surprise and something else Ezzy couldn't quite place. "The only time we see new faces 'round here is when the caravan comes through town."

"Syla Trane?" Ezzy didn't want to say anything until she was positive this was the woman she was looking for.

"Yes, that's me. How can I help you?"

"My name's Esmerelda Ciantar."

"Ciantar..." Syla looked like someone had walked over her grave. She took a step back, bumping into her tools and knocking them over. "I recognize you from the few times I visited your family home. Of course you were younger then. I can't believe you're here."

"My mother told me you could help me. We're looking for someone."

For a moment, Ezzy thought she would have to repeat herself. Syla stood there, staring at her, frozen by whatever was rattling around in her mind. Then the woman spoke.

"We shouldn't talk here. Come on back into my house. One of you, go lock the door first."

The woman left the room, exiting through the back door. Ezzy glanced at Nolan and received a shrug. Shayua was already sliding the latch into place. Ezzy wasn't sure what kind of reception she had expected, but this certainly was not it. She had already come this far though. Not the time to back down now just because of a feeling. Trying to leave her unease behind, Ezzy made her way through the back door.

A narrow hallway with wood paneling running down the walls contained a staircase to the right, leading up to the second floor. On the far end of the hall sat three doors, one straight ahead that probably led outside and one on each side. Syla was standing in the doorway on the left, waving Ezzy forward. Ezzy complied and found herself in the kitchen.

A small stove sat against the far corner as well as a few counter tops. A single table, just big enough for one, sat in the middle of the room along with a chair. A few racks suspended from the ceiling, but they were mostly empty. Everything made of metal in the room appeared brand new. The racks were free of dents and the surfaces of everything else gleamed like freshly polished silver.

"I don't have much to offer in terms of food and comfort, but I do have some tea from Wethrintir I can prepare."

"That sounds good," Ezzy said from the doorway. A nudge at her back signaled Nolan and Shayua's arrival. They shuffled into the room and stood around as Syla prepared the tea.

"I don't get many visitors," she said as she placed a pot on the stove and lit it. "I spend most of my time working, which leaves little time for being social."

"It's quite alright. Do you mind if my friend takes the chair? He has an injured knee."

"Feel free."

Nolan shuffled past her, whispering a "thank you" as he moved to the chair. Ezzy gave him a quick smile before returning her attention to Syla.

"If you don't mind me getting right to the point, we're trying to find someone and hope you could help."

"Your family has been so good to me over the years. Anything I can do to help you would be my pleasure. What is the person's name?"

"Iacane. I was told he had come to this village a while ago."

"Ah yes. The Saniteal. Sorry to be the one to tell you this, but he disappeared a few days ago."

"The Janpair family told me as much. I was hoping you might have an idea of what happened, or at least point us in the direction of where he was staying."

Syla continued to move about, straightening pots and pans, checking on the tea, picking up loose utensils. Not once had she met Ezzy's eyes since they had entered the kitchen. Ezzy found it off-putting, but then again, everyone that lived in this village seemed a little strange. Maybe it was normal here not to make eye contact when speaking to someone.

"Tea is ready." Syla grabbed four glasses off the counter and filled them from the pot. Passing them out, the woman couldn't hide behind preparing the tea and was forced to stop and talk to them. She stood there, shuffling in place, her eyes on the floor.

"So...uh, the Saniteal?" Ezzy asked. She took a sip of the tea. It was interesting, a mixture of sweet and sour. "What do you know?"

"I know he came because of the rumors about the Unyielding Wall, how it affects the people that live here in strange ways. All rumors, I assure you. I've lived here for a long time and haven't noticed anything strange."

"You also said you don't get out much."

"True, true. Anyway, this Saniteal had been around for a while, using his magic to examine each member of the village. I saw him a good amount when he was doing his rounds. Kept a notebook that he was always jotting something down in. He talked a lot too, sometimes even to himself. If you ask me, he's the strangest person in the village."

"But then he went missing? Do you think he annoyed enough people that he got chased out of the village? Or that something worse might have happened?"

"It's hard to be annoyed with a man that offered his healing services for free while he stayed in the village. I burned my hand a number of days ago, and he fixed me up in a matter of moments. Quite amazing, that magic of his."

"Well, if it wasn't because he was annoying the villagers, can you think of any other reason he might have disappeared? Even if it's something small, it might--"

She cut off as Nolan slid out of the chair, his empty cup cracking on the wood floor as he slumped to the ground.

"Nolan!" Moving to his side, she was relieved to find he was still breathing. He wouldn't wake up though when she shook him a few times. "Shayua, help me get him up. Shayua?"

Looking over her shoulder, Ezzy found Shayua looking at her with a confused expression. Then the tall woman's eyes rolled back in her head, and she crumpled to the floor as well.

"I'm sorry!" Syla said, taking a few steps back. "I don't know how they knew I had any relation with your family!"

"What? Who are you talking..." Ezzy's vision suddenly swam, the world around her turning hazy.

"They offered me money, which I rejected without a thought. But then they drew their weapons, started breaking things, even cut me a few times, until I agreed to help them. I didn't think you would actually show up. I didn't even think anyone in your family was still alive. I'm so sorry!"

Ezzy tried to put two thoughts together but failed. Her head grew heavy. A sharp pain broke through the haze for a moment as her head hit the ground.

Then blackness.

Chapter Twenty-Three

A Darkening Mind

Panic. That's the emotion Nolan felt as he woke up, face down on a stone floor, hands bound behind his back. Rolling to his side, he saw an empty room with dark grey, stone walls devoid of any windows. A thick wooden door was the only way in or out. A single candle sat in a sconce in each corner of the room, well above his reach. The flames flickered about, as if they also wanted to escape the dank room.

Any movement on his part sent jagged bolts of lightning through his injured shoulder. Even so, with a great deal of effort, he managed to sit upright. From a sitting position, it took a little more effort for him to struggle to his feet.

Now what?

The blacksmith had drugged them, that much was clear. He could be in her basement. Were Ezzy and Shayua somewhere nearby? If the blacksmith knew anything about Ezzy, their captor would have to keep her drugged to make sure she didn't bring Paz in to free them all. Unless they had gotten her far enough away from Paz that she couldn't control him. Had he been out long enough for them to travel that far? The room he was in gave away nothing. Nolan could have been asleep for a whole season for all he knew.

Limping about, he tried to find anything that might give him a clue as to what was going on or how he could escape. Whoever his captor was, they had done an excellent job of clearing the room. He couldn't even find a random rock or piece of the wall that had broken off to use as a tool to cut his binds. Even though getting his hands free wouldn't help him at all, it would ease his discomfort somewhat. At least it would lessen the pain of the ropes rubbing his wrists raw. Maybe if he tried pounding on the door, someone would come and tell him what was going on and maybe loosen--

The door. Or more specifically, the door hinges.

The door sat on a wooden frame held in place by three hinges evenly spaced. It opened inward, meaning the hinges were also on the inside of the room. Backing up against the door frame, he began rubbing his bindings as hard as he could against one of the protruding hinges. He pinched his skin quite a few times as he sawed into the ropes, but he felt them start to give. It might take him a while, but Nolan believed he could eventually get through his bindings. The process gave him some time to reflect on how he got here.

How had he let his life come to this? He had a well decorated home, a variety of expensive and comfortable clothes, and enough money saved up and hidden away that he could lock himself in his house and only come out to buy supplies and pick up a few books to read and live happily. As he had gotten older, that had been all he wanted. That, and to retire before he completely lost his mind. Now, he was locked in a room and who knew what his future held? All because of one girl.

Ezzy.

Sure he had argued against the idea of hunting this Ean fellow down, but when she showed no sign of budging, he had agreed to go without giving it another thought. Why? Of course she meant something to him. He had watched her grow up; he was like an uncle to her. But why hadn't he tried talking her out of seeking her own form of justice for her father, whatever it might be? Had he wanted a measure of redemption as well for his old employer and friend? A part of him knew that no matter what he said, Ezzy was too headstrong to let go of the past. Did he go along with her just to watch over her? Or was it to make sure she didn't do something she would regret? Why couldn't he answer his own questions?

A dimming of the light made him look up. Deep in thought, he had stopped working at the ropes. Why had it gotten darker? There weren't any windows in the room. He looked up at the candles and what he saw made him groan. The candles, which had been easily a hand-length long when he woke, were almost completely melted down.

It had happened again. Lost in his thoughts, what had seemed like moments had been much, much longer. So much time had been lost all because he couldn't stop his mind from wandering. *Focus, Nolan.* He began sawing at the ropes around his wrist even faster, trying to make up for all of the lost time. His muscles burned from the effort, and he expected to feel blood dripping down his wrists as raw skin finally broke. But he had to work harder. He might only get one chance to escape and he wouldn't have much of a chance with his hands bound behind his back.

"Focus, Nolan," he whispered. "For your and Ezzy's sake."

And possibly Shayua's, but she was low on the importance scale compared to Ezzy. And the woman could handle herself. She had probably escaped and was working to free them already. That would be nice. Nolan could just sit and wait...

Darkness descended on the room like a curtain.

"Not again..."

The candles' flames were gone along with what little light they had provided. A meager glow spread out from beneath the door, barely lighting the boots on his feet. Nolan pressed himself against the door. He hated being in a pitch-black room, regardless of whether it was his bedroom or a cell. The darkness seemed to press down on him. Crush him. He heard the scratching of animals coming from the walls and moving across the floor. He needed to get out of there.

Fueled by fear, Nolan began fervently working at his restraints again. He didn't care anymore how badly he sliced up his wrists. He wanted his hands free. Needed them free. What if whatever was crawling around tried to crawl onto him? Get into his clothes? Claw its way up his skin?

Nolan tripled his efforts.

By the time Nolan heard the satisfying snap of the ropes coming free, his hands were dripping with sweat.

No, that metallic smell isn't sweat.

Lifting his hands up in front of his face, he could barely see a tint of red covering his skin. How badly had he injured his wrists? They felt raw to his touch, and wet, but his skin wasn't spurting blood. Nolan took a few deep, calming breaths. The darkness still threatened to smother him, but just having his hands free seemed to help. He no longer heard the scratching of claws on stone. Had it been his mind playing tricks on him? His mind did a lot of things now that he had no control over.

Another sound caught his ear. Boots on stone. Someone was coming.

Nolan bent down, searching for the discarded ropes. A shockwave of pain raced through his body as his knee knocked into the wall. He found the rope just as he heard the clinking sound of a key going into a lock. Scrambling away from the door, he ended up rolling onto his side in the middle of the room just as the click of the lock disengaging echoed in the room. Nolan tried to ignore the pain bouncing around his body as the door opened and a man entered.

"Ah, my mistake." He sounded young, but with what little light entered the room coming from behind him, Nolan couldn't make anything else out about the man. "Didn't mean to let the light go out. I fell asleep."

Nolan didn't feel the need to respond to his captor. Looking through the door, all he could see was a dimly lit stone corridor. He remained motionless as the man moved over to the nearest candleholder and put in a new candle.

"We don't want to treat you like this, of course, but we have to be careful." He lit the candle and moved onto the next one. "You worked for the Ciantar family for a long time. It's understandable you feel some kind of loyalty to them. I'm sure they paid you a great deal of money over the years."

With the second candle lit and some light returning to the room, Nolan was able to make out a bit more about the man. Nothing special jumped out at him at first. Plain clothes covered an average-sized man. His more than shoulder-length brown hair was tied behind his head. A plain face with no distinguishable marks glanced at him for a moment, then moved on to the next sconce. Nolan rolled around, both to keep his eyes on the man and to keep his captor from seeing his hands were free. It was when the man reached the fourth candleholder that Nolan noticed the color of the man's clothes. His dark green shirt clashed with his maroon pants.

And a band of orange hung from his waist.

"You're part of the Orange Hound Gang."

He let out a laugh. "It's the clothes that give it away, right? Our leader takes great pride in our outfits. I think it's foolish to make it so obvious whom we work for, but you won't catch me saying that to his face. I value my life too much to go running my mouth around him or any of the other higher-ups of the gang."

"Where is Ezzy?"

"She's fine."

"Can you be a bit more specific?"

"They are keeping her asleep. Don't want that metal giant of hers causing any problems until we can load you all into the wagons and take you back to Wethrintir."

"What? Why are we going there?"

"Oh, wasn't supposed to mention that...ah, by the Abyss, I guess it doesn't matter if I tell you. Just act surprised when my the man in charge of our crew comes in to talk to you."

"Ok." Nolan would say anything to keep the man talking.

"Well, the Big Boss is situated in Wethrintir. Controls quite a bit of the homes and stores there. Our numbers grow every day, and we have members in every village and city, except Rottwealth, of course. Impossible to get anyone into that backward village."

"What does that have to do with us?"

"Well, the boss has taken a bit of interest in you three. Probably because you've messed with his men so much. He's been interested in Esmerelda since her Vilathos punched all those holes in his town. You can't get away with doing that without there being consequences."

"So this is purely motivated by revenge?"

"Well, I wouldn't say that. The boss could have had us torture and kill her here. Would have still sent the same message. He might still do that with that crimson freak of a woman. She doesn't really hold much value to our group."

"But Ezzy and I do?"

"Well, like I said, I'm not very high in the pecking order, but I have heard enough to put a few things together. Esmerelda is a prominent person in the realm, even with her family falling so far. She might still have some worth. She is certainly pretty enough to be put to work, if you know what I mean. After they break that stubborn spirit of hers. You're the real prize, though."

"Me? Why me?"

"Because you're a Thaljori. And a good one from what the men have learned about you. It's not like there are hundreds of your kind either. The few of you that exist all reside in Lurthalan, rarely leave the city, and most of you would be noticed if you went missing. It's almost impossible to snatch one of you up right when your powers first start to show. Our boss has failed at recruiting any of the established Thaljori in the realm as well. That makes you very valuable."

"You mean I'm being held here because he wants to hire me?"

"Seems that way."

"Well, you can tell him or whoever you report to that I'm retired."

"I wouldn't make any decisions yet. You have the whole trip back to Wethrintir to think it over. Ben can be quite persuasive."

"Ben? Is that the same man that's been chasing us all over the realm?"

"The one and the same. He was put in charge of our little group sent to bring you in. I can't even begin to tell you how frustrated you've made him. Ben came storming into town, swearing up a storm about the three of you. Especially that monster of a woman. I've found Ben to be a patient man, probably part of the reason he has risen in the ranks so fast, but getting shot with an arrow will test any man's temper. Your friend might not make it to Wethrintir, if you catch my meaning."

"We're hardly friends..."

"Oh? Well anyway, like I was saying, I wouldn't get too set on turning down our boss. You might not like the crimson one that much, but he knows you are close to the Ciantar family. He might keep Esmerelda around just to use her as leverage to get you to work for him. And he likes removing people's fingers, just as a warning. It's his thing, I guess, to stand out among the other gang leaders."

"He better not touch her. None of you better even lay a finger on her."

"See? You get all worked up over just the mention of hurting her. Might as well just accept the fact you'll be working for the Orange Hounds. I'm sure if you do as you're told, you will be rewarded handsomely."

Nolan glared at the man. The way he could so casually talk about hurting Ezzy sickened him. This thug...no, everyone associated with the Orange Hounds, were nothing but monsters.

"Well," the man said, moving towards the door. "Someone will bring you some food later. The wagons should get here by tomorrow, so until then, this room will be your...wait a tick. What's this?"

Kneeling by the door, the man knelt and examined the floor. When his hand was raised, a red tint was clear on his fingers.

"You hurt? I can't have you making a mess of yourself." He gave Nolan a quick looking over. "Stand up. Let me take a better look at you."

Not knowing what else to do, Nolan stood.

"Turn around. Let me see your hands."

Nolan stood still.

"Come on, old man. Don't make this difficult. Our orders are to not hurt you much. That leaves a lot of freedom to decide how much is much."

Nolan shrugged. Not much else he could do. Spreading his arms wide, he let the man see the damage he had done to his wrists getting free.

"Well, you're more resourceful than we all thought. That's a shame though. I'm going to have to tie your hands again. The rope certainly won't feel good on those wrists now. Maybe we can get that looked at tonight."

Nolan took a step back. This would probably be his only chance to escape, except the man in front of him was younger, stronger, and probably knew how to fight. Nolan didn't even have a weapon to flail about wildly at the man. His shoulder burned and his knee ached to the point he could barely keep much weight on it. Still, he had to try.

"Listen," the man took a step towards him, "I'll try to leave it as loose as I can without it being easy for you to slip out or get the knots loose. Best I can do."

Nolan took another step back.

"I swear, though, if you try to fight me in this, I'll make you regret it."

Nolan's back hit the wall.

"See? Nowhere to go. Now just stick your hands out--"

Nolan threw a punch.

It wasn't the most well executed attack, but he had watched Ezzy get in enough scraps to at least put a little power into it.

It glanced off the man's shoulder. The expression on his face was more of disappointment than pain.

The punch the man threw, on the other hand, struck Nolan square in the chest. He stumbled backwards and struck the wall, his knees buckling as the breath left his body.

"Now don't make me hit you again. I feel bad hitting an old man. Doesn't mean I won't knock a few of your teeth free, but I'll feel bad doing it."

Nolan lashed out a kick. It hit the man's shin, making him stumble a step. He retaliated with a back hand that rattled Nolan's teeth but didn't knock any free.

"Now I'm getting annoyed." Gripping Nolan's shirt, the man lifted him off the ground and slammed him against the wall. "If it will be easier to tie you up while you are unconscious, I have no problem with that."

Nolan grabbed the man's arm and tried to pull it off him, but he wasn't even strong enough to give it a good shake.

Another backhand almost succeeded in knocking him out, but he held on. Barely. Held up by the man, his eyes closed from the pain, Nolan wanted to just give in. Sleep was certainly better than lying awake on a stone floor. Peaceful sleep.

Then he thought of Ezzy.

Nolan wasn't sure what made him reach out with his magic. Maybe it was frustration at being so useless. Or it could have been desperation. In the end it didn't matter. He found the other man's consciousness. Felt the energy of his mind. It flowed through his incorporeal grasp like a gentle breeze.

He gripped it and tore it from the man.

The Orange Hound member's grip dropped away. His whole body dropped away. The gang member slumped to the ground, his eyes wide and blank.

Nolan had done something no one else in history had ever done before.

He had used his magic as a Thaljori to kill.

Chapter Twenty-Four

HIDE AND SEEK

The reality of what Nolan had done rocked him more than any of the blows he had received.

He had taken a life.

He had taken a life using his magic.

Nolan stood there, in his cell, with the door to his freedom sitting wide open. He couldn't move. He could barely breathe.

When creating Vilathos, accidents could happen with deadly results. He had lost people before in the dangerous process. Some people had died, others had lost their minds, and some had even been lost *in* their minds. But those people knew the risks, knew a variety of things could go wrong. Nolan always felt bad for the man or woman when it happened, and he tried his hardest not to let it happen, but sometimes things were out of his control. He had never dwelt on the lives that had been lost during the process.

But this was different. He had deliberately reached out and tore apart the man's mind.

A churning started in his stomach. Moved up to his throat.

"By the gods..." he managed to get out before bending over and throwing up on the floor.

With his stomach emptied and his body still sore from the beating he had received, Nolan tried to stand. Dizziness washed over him. He stumbled to the side, his shoulder slamming into the wall. The new pain mixed with the old.

"What have I done..."

All of the temples in Lurthalan saw the taking of life as an executable offense. Taking a life through the use of magic warranted an even worse punishment, although he had no idea what was worse than death. The law just stated the punishment was worse and anyone accused disappeared soon after. He could claim self-defense, but the laws written down by the temples applied differently when magic was involved. And as far as he knew, he was the first ever to use his type of magic to kill. Would they have to create new laws because of him?

But that was the future. He needed to focus on the here and now.

Ezzy and Shayua. They needed him.

"Focus."

Nolan was surprised to find that just that one word snapped his mind back into the present. It was more than that though. That haze that so often tried to cloud his thoughts was gone. He felt energized as well, sore of course, but energized. Had something happened when he had killed the man?

"Get moving," he whispered to himself.

He was out the door and glancing around in a heartbeat, despite his bad knee. The hallway ran straight ahead and a side hallway went to his left. Down either direction, doors similar to the one that had kept him caged sat closed. Nolan was about to call out for his companions but thought better of it. No one knew he was free. It could be a while before anyone even came down to check on them. Best not to waste that advantage.

So, which way?

Ezzy would be kept as deep into this place as possible. That idea made him choose to go left. There was only one door in sight in this direction, and he moved toward it and pushed.

It didn't budge.

Of course, it's going to be locked, you fool.

Moving as quiet as he could, Nolan returned to his own cell. He needed the keys the man he killed carried, but that meant he had to look at the man he had killed.

The body lay in the same spot where it had fallen. His legs were folded up beneath his body and his arms were splayed out at weird angles. Trickles of blood dripped out of his ears and nose. The worst thing was his eyes. They had turned a crimson red. Even with the pupils gone, the lifeless stare felt like an accusation.

Murderer. Butcher. Killer.

It took him a moment, but Nolan pushed away the guilt. The man could have been all of those things and probably more. Who knows what he had done in the past, the people he had hurt? Nolan shouldn't feel bad about defending himself.

As he removed the keys from the guard's belt, a thumping sound down the hall startled him to attention. The keys fumbled to the floor with a clatter. Nolan silently cursed and froze in place, listening until he was confident that his clumsiness had gone unheard. Snatching up the keys, he left the room and returned to the solitary door down the hallway. The lock clicked open without a problem, allowing Nolan to push the door open and enter the room. A cell that mirrored his own greeted Nolan as he entered. It was completely empty except for one thing.

The prisoner inside.

Disappointment washed over Nolan. The prisoner rose as Nolan entered. The rags of what used to be a shirt and pants hung from his stocky build. Thinning black hair, matted with dirt, framed the face of a man that looked to be close to Nolan in age. Fear shone through the man's brown eyes and his lips trembled. He started to shake as Nolan took another step into the room, and he grasped his bound hands in front of his body.

"Please, no more! I can't take any more."

"Quiet," Nolan whispered, raising his hands in a calming manner. "I'm not one of them. I was locked up as well but escaped."

"What do you take me for, a fool? A thin man like you taking down one of those thugs on your own? What game are you playing? Are you supposed to be the gentle approach after days of those others beating me silly? I'm too intelligent to fall for something so obvious."

"I don't have time for this."

Nolan turned his back on the man and walked out the door. Glancing to his left he noticed a passage and the beginning of a stairwell at the end of the hall he had missed before. Go up or search the other rooms down here? The choice was obvious to his focused mind. It only made sense that his companions would be down here as well. His captors wouldn't risk holding prisoners upstairs where they could call out or make a break for the front door. More likely than not, there were guards stationed at the top of the stairs as well. He would continue to search on this level. Stepping away from the room, he was about to move towards the first door on the left when a hand grabbed his arm.

"Let's say you are a prisoner like me," the stocky man said. "Shouldn't we be moving to those steps? The faster we can get out of here, the better in my opinion."

"I have other friends that I believe are being kept here."

"All the more reason to escape. It will be easier for just the two of us to sneak out of here. I'm pretty well known in the area, and I'm sure the Janpair family would swoop in here and get rid of these ruffians once they find out how I've been treated. They'll free your friends."

"I'm not leaving them here." Pulling his arm free, Nolan moved down the hall. The stocky man was quick to follow.

"This really is foolish. I don't know how you were lucky enough to get free, but there could be dozens of men stationed above us. Are you some kind of skilled warrior? You certainly don't look it, but I doubt you could take a dozen or so men. Unless you are an Elementalist? I'd even take a Sparkteller at this point."

"I'm a Thaljori."

"Ah, then you're just as useless as I am when it comes to a fight. I'm a Saniteal by the way. Iacane Brill, you might have heard of me."

So, that's where the man they had been looking for had disappeared to.

"Yes, I've heard of you, but not for the reasons you're probably thinking."

Iacane let out a nervous laugh. "But you have heard of me. That's what matters."

"If you say so."

They had reached the first door. *Please let Ezzy be inside.* Another lock slowed him down, but his key worked in it as well. He stepped inside the room with baited breath.

I find everyone except who I want to find.

The candles had dwindled down in the room, leaving the light in the hall the only bit that showed Shayua's tied up form. She sat in a chair, her head down, hair covering her face, and her chin on her chest. Her arms were behind her back, probably tied there, and Nolan could see the ropes that tied her ankles to the legs of the chair. She didn't raise her head as he entered. The warrior was probably plotting some kind of escape.

"What kind of a..." Iacane began but Nolan cut him off.

"She's a very dangerous bounty hunter you should not anger. Now be quiet." Nolan strode towards Shayua and knelt in front of her. "Shayua, it's me Nolan. Shayua?"

The woman didn't respond. Nolan slowly put a hand to her shoulder, hoping she didn't bite it off, and gave her a shake. She remained limp. Against his better judgment, he gently grasped her chin and brushed the hair out of her face.

Shayua looked like she had been trampled by a herd of horses. Her face was bruised and cut. One of her eyes was swollen shut. Her nose was broken in at least two places. A particularly nasty gash ran along the left side of her chin. The bounty hunter was breathing, but the air wheezed out of her mouth and nose.

"Iacane. You have to heal her."

Walking up to Nolan's side, the Saniteal bent down and examined Shay. After a few moments, he shook his head.

"She's too badly hurt."

"What? I thought people with your skill could heal much, much worse?"

"We can," he growled. "I can. But if I heal her completely, she'll be out for a while as her body recovers from the process, and I'll be in even worse shape. Think you can sneak out of here while carrying the two of us?"

"No, I..." He wanted to punch something. Punch Iacane, even if the man was telling the truth. Nolan really didn't know much about how a Saniteal's power worked. No one with any real magical power associated with people of different talents. By the Abyss, he never socialized with other Thaljori.

"Well, we can't just leave her here. Is there something you can do?"

"Move." The scared tone was gone, replaced by a steel that Nolan hadn't expected from the man. "Let me take a closer look."

Iacane crouched down again in front of Shay and placed both of his hands on the sides of her head. He remained there, eyes closed for what felt like forever. Nolan kept glancing at the door, expecting their captors to stride in at any moment and make them pay for trying to get away.

"I can wake her up, help her enough that she can move on her own. Just don't expect much else out of her. Help me get these ropes off of her first."

"Let's leave her tied up at least until she recognizes me. I don't want there to be any misunderstandings."

"Is she really that dangerous?"

"From what little I've seen of her in action. She tried to go head-to-head with a metal Vilathos twice her size."

"Yes, let's leave her tied then. Alright, hold on."

Iacane closed his eyes and grew still. Nolan had never seen a Saniteal at work before and had no idea what to expect. Right away sweat began to bead on his forehead. His face twitched. His body began to shake, and he let out a small moan. Nolan gasped as a small slash appeared on the man's chin and then disappeared. Did healing a person mess with a Saniteal's body in a similar way that creating a Vilathos damaged a Thaljori's mind?

With a gasp, Iacane fell backwards. He lay on the floor staring at the ceiling, his breaths coming in ragged gasps.

"Did it work? Is she alright?"

"Give me a moment. I did what I could. She had a few injuries inside of her body that I had to fix. Those take a lot out of me. You should be able to wake her up though."

"Thank you."

Nolan gave the woman's shoulder a shake.

"Shay. I need you to wake up. It's Nolan."

Shay lifted her head. Her one eye was still swollen shut, but her face was less bruised and the gash on her chin had closed. She glanced around, her gaze resting on Iacane for a moment before it ended on Nolan.

"Where is Esmerelda?"

"I don't know; we haven't found her yet. They are keeping her drugged."

"Is this man one of the ones that took us?"

"No, he was a prisoner as well. He healed you."

"Wonderful. Another man I owe. Why am I still bound?"

"Just making sure you didn't kill me by accident when you woke."

"A smart move. You may untie me now though, Nolan."

It took him longer than he expected to loosen the ropes. They had tied her as tight as possible to the chair. He couldn't blame them. If he had wanted to tie Shay up, he would have used chains just to make sure. When she was free, Shay rose to her feet on wobbly legs.

"I'm surprised you can even stand," Iacane said from the floor. "That much healing would keep a weaker person in bed for half a day at the least."

"I am not weak. Do you need me to carry you to prove it?"

"No, no." Iacane sat up, although he struggled to do it. "Last thing we need is you trying to show off and dropping me when your legs give out. Just try to conserve what strength you have. I'm sure you'll need it if we're going to escape."

"Fine. Let's find Ezzy."

Not waiting for the two men, Shay moved towards the door.

"Go right," Nolan called to her. "There is a door that way we haven't checked yet."

Shay nodded before turning the corner and moving out of sight.

"A pleasant woman," Iacane said, getting to his feet. "What exactly is she? When I healed her, she felt human, but there was also something else there."

"She's part Shadaer. Something you should not bring up. Shayua is very sensitive about her past. Now let's go before she decides to try and take on our captors instead of trying to escape."

"She would try that? Even in her condition?"

The sound of splintering wood echoed outside the room. Rushing back into the hallway, Nolan saw Shayua to his right entering into the room at the end of the hall. Pieces of the door lay scattered about.

"How did she break through one of those doors?" Iacane was at his side. "She should barely be able to stand!"

"Your guess is as good as mine. She is a very determined woman."

Reaching the door, Nolan looked inside and a weight lifted off of his shoulders. There was Ezzy, asleep on top of a pile of straw. Shayua was at her side. Then he heard shouts coming from back towards the stairs.

Chapter Twenty-Five

ESCAPE

Everyone froze as the muffled sound of voices reached them. Nolan knew they only had moments before whoever it was realized something was wrong. With Shayua injured, he doubted they could take on more than two or three people at a time. They had to come up with an idea. HE had to come up with an idea.

"Iacane. Can you wake Ezzy? They knocked her out with some kind of drug."

"Possibly. I can cleanse her the same way I would a poison. It would knock me out though. Then I would be useless in helping us escape."

"This girl is connected to a Vilathos. Who do you think would be better in a fight? You or a metal Vilathos?"

"I understand."

While Iacane moved to Ezzy's side, Nolan turned his attention to Shayua.

"How are you feeling?"

"I can fight."

"Shayua, that's not what I asked. How are you feeling?"

The tall bounty hunter tried to put on a brave face for a moment longer, then her expression fell.

"I feel like I've been beaten from the inside out, but don't worry about me, I can handle a few thugs." Shay picked up a piece of the broken door that still had a few nails sticking out of it. She gave it a few swings. "This will do."

"Hopefully there aren't a dozen men then."

"How did you escape?" Shay asked.

The question caught him off guard. Nolan's focus wavered for a moment as the memory of killing the man flashed through his mind. Then it was gone.

"A story for another time. Preferably in an inn, surrounded by food and drink, and not under attack."

"Sounds like a boring night to me." A half smile formed on the woman's lips. Nolan felt a small amount of reassurance from Shayua's confidence. A very small amount. If there were a dozen or so men down here...

A thud behind him made Nolan spin. He found Iacane on the ground, a bit of drool coming out of his mouth. Ezzy didn't show any sign of waking up. Blasted Saniteal! Had he made a mistake somehow?

A shout sounded from somewhere out in the hall. They had run out of time. Moving to Ezzy's side, Nolan began to shake her shoulders. He started gently at first, but as desperation sank in he grew more and more rough. As more shouts began to echo down the hall, he gave up on being nice.

"Forgive me," he whispered before slapping Ezzy's face.

Her eyes fluttered but she remained still. Grimacing, Nolan hit her again.

Ezzy's eyes shot open for a moment, then slowly began to shut again.

"Sleep..." she mumbled. "Little more..."

"Nope."

Grabbing Ezzy's shoulders he lifted her up to a sitting position. Her eyes began to droop, so he tapped her cheek a few times until she opened her eyes.

"Ezzy, we don't have a lot of time."

"What's going on?" Her words were slurred and her eyes kept dropping. Had Iacane not gotten the drug out of her system completely?

"No time for that. Can you feel Paz?"

"Of course. Like a rope around my brain, pulling me..."

"Wonderful. Get him here. NOW."

"But I don't--"

"Ezzy, we're in danger. Get him here now!"

"Ok, ok. It's on the way."

But would it get here in time?

"Men are coming," Shayua said from the doorway. Her head was barely peeking around the corner. "I count four. I might be able to take four."

"Don't you dare go running off to fight," Nolan hissed at her. "You'll have a better chance if they have to come at you through the doorway."

"I know this, Nolan. You worry about your magic, and I'll worry about the fighting."

Insufferable woman. She was their only defense though. Nolan still had to hold Ezzy up, Iacane was snoring on the floor, and as for himself...

He could kill again if he needed to do it. It was simple. Just grab a man's consciousness and pull. Nolan had to touch the man for it to work, but that shouldn't be hard to do while the man was beating him down. As long as he could get a good hold, killing would be as easy as pulling up a blade of grass.

And that terrified him.

Terrified and thrilled him. And the fact that killing a man had a positive effect on his own mental condition...

"Here they come."

Shayua backed away from the door. Laying Ezzy back down on the table, Nolan moved to pick up another piece of the door. It wasn't as balanced as his walking staff, but it would do. He might not be the best fighter, but he would do his best to fend the men off. And if he had to use his magic...

A man in dirty clothes and an orange headband burst through the doorway. Shayua dropped him with one swing. A second, similarly dressed man stopped at the doorway and drew his sword before entering.

"They're all in here," he shouted, then lunged at Shay.

She deflected the blade with her makeshift club. The sword shaved a chunk out of the wood, but Shay held tight. The thug stabbed at her twice more then tried an overhand swing. Shay parried all three, then moved in and grabbed the man by the throat. There was a crunching sound and the man went limp.

Shayua tossed the man and her club to the side then picked up his discarded blade. She hefted it in her hand a few times, then smiled.

"Much better."

Two more men appeared at the door. Glancing at their fallen brothers, they smartly remained outside.

"Go get more of the men. Tell them all of the prisoners are free. I'll hold them here 'til you return."

Shayua barked a laugh as one of the men ran off. "You will hold us here? I think not."

"We'll see." The man drew a curved blade with wicked-looking notches along the edge. "Come get me then, you freak."

Shayua crossed the distance between them in a heartbeat. Their blades met with a clash. Shayua advanced through the door, leaving Nolan with the slumbering Iacane and the barely awake Ezzy.

Should I try to help or will I just get in the way? Probably the latter.

Keeping his club in hand, Nolan moved to Ezzy's side. If their captors were getting more men, their only chance would be Paz. Unfortunately Ezzy's eyes were closed and she wore a contented smile. If she had gotten Paz moving before nodding off again, they would be alright. A Vilathos always followed its last command as long as its owner was still alive. If she had told him Paz was on the way just so he would let her go back to sleep, though, they were in a lot of trouble.

"Ezzy." He gave her a shake. "Ezzy, wake back up. Come on."

She mumbled something and tried to roll over onto her side. Nolan held her on place and shook her again. Outside of the room, he heard the repeated clang of metal-on-metal.

"Ezzy, get up. We're running out of time."

She lazily swung a hand to try and bat him away. He caught it and hooked his arm underneath her shoulder, then lifted her back into a sitting position. Then he began to violently shake her until she opened her eyes.

"By the Abyss, Nolan. What do you--"

Shayua tumbled backwards through the doorway, her sword skittering across the floor. The man she had been dueling with entered right behind her, his sword still in hand. He also wore the smirk of a man winning a fight.

"Shay!"

The sight of her mentor seemed to snap Ezzy awake. She hopped off the table onto unsteady legs and took a few steps towards Shay until the man turned his sword in her direction.

"Stop right there," he growled. "I'll take a slice out of each of ya' if you don't be good little captives. The boss wants you alive, but that doesn't mean he needs you in one piece."

"There is only one of you--" Ezzy began, but the man cut her off.

"I can take a bruised up freak, two old men, and a spoiled ex-rich girl without breaking a sweat."

Seeing Shay on the ground, Nolan started to think the man might not be bluffing. Shayua looked tired and was sporting a few new cuts on her arms. Her opponent seemed comfortable with the sword in his hand, and wasn't even breathing heavily. It didn't look good. How far away was Paz?

"Ezzy, maybe we should listen..."

"Shay," Ezzy said. "Get up. We can take him together."

"Sure," the man said with a laugh. "Try to take me. I guarantee I'll kill the red beast. And if you die too...well, accidents happen. We'll still have the Thaljori and Saniteal."

Shayua at this point had gotten to her feet and was moving towards her fallen sword. The man watched her move then pointed to the sword.

"Go ahead. Pick it up. I've killed plenty of women before, what's two more?"

Shay did as she was told. Ezzy had picked up a piece of the door at some point and held it ready. Both woman spread out, circling the man. He stood there as if he was watching grass grow. He even went so far as to let out a sigh. Shayua snarled at him.

"You will regret your insults, cretin, when this sword is stuck in your belly."

"We'll see."

The man made a feint at Ezzy, causing her to stumble backwards, then advanced on Shayua.

Their battle was like a beautifully rehearsed dance. Shay caught his first swing with a well-placed parry and immediately followed up with a strike of her own. He twisted out of its way, ending his turn by thrusting his blade at Shay's stomach. She blocked that strike as well, then dropped and tried to sweep his legs. He stepped back out of reach before advancing on her again.

Back and forth they went, the sound of clashing steel, their footsteps on the wooden floor, and their breaths the only sound in the room. Nolan had never seen two people skilled with the sword battle before. Even Ezzy seemed mesmerized by the dance playing out before them.

Until the man caught Shay with a slight cut to her sword arm.

With a yell, Ezzy charged into the fight, club in hand. Which warned the man of her attack. He disengaged Shay, taking a few steps back. When Ezzy reached him, she swung her club wildly. He avoided each swing with a laugh. That smile disappeared, though, when Shayua moved in to attack as well.

Dodging one of Ezzy's swings and then deflecting a thrust from Shay, the man's face furrowed in concentration. Nolan watched as sweat started to appear on his brow and create stains in his clothes. His swings became less controlled, his parries barely keeping Shay's blade and Ezzy's club from connecting. The women were winning!

A shout from somewhere outside the room destroyed what little hope had started to build in Nolan's stomach. More men were coming.

Shayua seemed to ignore the sound, but it distracted Ezzy enough that she paused her attacks.

The man struck, catching Ezzy with a well-placed kick to her stomach. The blow knocked her backwards, and she lost her grip on the club as she hit the floor. Shay attacked with a fervor, but with only one person to worry about now, the man's superior skill started to show again. He blocked her attacks with ease. Then, as Shay took a reckless swing, the man caught her blade in the notches on the back of his sword, twisted his wrist, and yanked the blade from Shay's hand. The momentum carried Shay forward, right into a perfectly placed left hook. The blow rocked Shay and she crumpled to the ground as her legs lost their strength. Standing over the fallen bounty hunter, the man rested the tip of his blade on her throat.

"There, it's over," he said, panting. "Don't make me kill you."

"Ok, stop." Ezzy said, still on the ground. "Don't hurt her. We surrender."

"No, Ezzy," Shayua glared at the girl. "You can't. They will never let any of us go. Best to die a good death now than to be slaves forever."

"A lot of things can happen from now 'til forever, Shay."

"Exactly," the man chimed in. "Listen to your friend. Your little group might have annoyed 'ole Ben to no end, but those above him are certainly curious about you. Which is why we haven't killed you yet. Your 'forever' might involve a life or riches and power if you join our group."

"I will not work for a bunch of thugs and bullies!" Shayua went to stand but the tip of the man's sword kept her in place.

"Then they will probably kill you. Maybe torture you first and make an example of you. Either way, the Orange Hounds will get something out of you."

"Which is why," Ezzy said, getting to her feet, "we surrender."

"Good. Now as soon as more of the Hounds get down here, we'll tie you back up and--"

Another shout from outside of the room interrupted him for a moment.

"I have everything under control!" Moving to the doorway, he peeked outside. "I just need a few men and some rope to tie them up!"

More muffled yells, this time coming from above them. The thud of boots on the floorboards above them rained dirt down between the cracks between the pieces of wood.

"What are they doing up there?" the man mumbled. "Bunch of drunks. Sometimes I wonder why I joined up with--"

A loud boom shook the floorboards above them, raining dust and dirt down on the room. The shouts from upstairs cut off. Then another boom shook even the stone walls around them. The yelling resumed as crashes echoed from every direction at once. The floor thumped as if a stamped was charging through the building.

"I think you should go see what that's all about," Ezzy shouted over the commotion above.

"Shut up! I'm not letting you out of my sight."

"If you say so." Ezzy took a few steps back. "Shay, would you mind backing up a bit?"

The man raised his sword towards the bounty hunter.

"You stay right there. I'm the one in charge here. No one is going to move unless I tell you to!"

"Shay! Now!"

Shay rolled away from the man. He took a step after her, then the ceiling directly above him exploded downward in a rain of wood and nails.

Followed by the enormous metal body of Paz.

Chapter Twenty-Six

No Longer Welcome

Paz hit the ground hard, his metal feet cracking the stone floor. Ezzy couldn't help but laugh at the expression on their captor's face at the sight of her metal construct.

Then she had Paz backhand him.

The blow knocked the man into the air and out the door.

"Not so cocky now, are you?" Ezzy mumbled before going to check on Shayua. "You ok?"

"My pride is the only thing badly wounded."

Climbing to her feet, she picked up a sword before glancing at what was left of the ceiling. Shaking her head, she moved over and tapped Paz a few times with her blade.

"I suppose your metal monster does have its uses."

"Why are we wasting time?" Iacane said, moving towards the door. "We should get out of here now."

"I agree," Nolan added.

"Fine, let's go." Ezzy affectionately patted her Vilathos as she moved towards the door. She knew it didn't have any kind of sentience, but she liked imagining sometimes that it did. Having Paz around had gotten them out of trouble plenty of times, and this had certainly been the worst. Being bound to him had been the best decision she had ever made.

And Paz had been the last gift her father had given her before his death.

Entering the hall, Ezzy found the swordsman slumped on the ground against the far wall. A small line of blood dribbled out of his mouth, but he was still breathing. She felt little pity for how he would feel when he woke up.

The others joined her outside the room, and they made their way down the hall. The building was eerily quiet, besides Paz's heavy footfalls on the stone floor. Ezzy couldn't tell if the lack of noise from above was a good thing or a bad one. Had their captives fled, or were they lying in wait upstairs? Well, only one way to find out.

Reaching the stairs, Shayua pushed to the front of their group. "I'll go first. Unless you want to send Paz up ahead of us."

Glancing at the narrow stairway leading up, Ezzy shook her head. "He won't fit that way. I'll have to send him back and see if he can climb out on his own back through the ceiling."

"Then I'll take the lead. Leave some space behind me."

As Paz marched away, the rest of their group crept up the stone stairs. Shay took the lead, followed by Ezzy, Nolan, and Iacane at the rear. Shadows danced around the narrow hallway and a door sat slightly ajar at the peak. Not a single sound could be heard from upstairs. When they reached the door, Shay glanced around the corner.

"All clear, except the path of destruction Paz left behind. We should get outside before this building crumbles."

They moved out of the stairway. Shayua hadn't been exaggerating. A hole, slightly larger than Paz, went from the outside wall thru what looked like what was left of a kitchen, and ended in the room they were entering. A large hole in the floor sat square in the middle of the room, with Paz standing at the bottom of it.

"Can it climb out?" Nolan asked at her side.

"Probably, but it might do even more damage to the building. We should be outside when it tries, just to be on the safe side."

"I just want to be out in the sun," Iacane said. The man pushed pass them, almost knocking Nolan into the hole. "I've been trapped down in that room for days. I need some fresh air."

"Pleasant fellow," Nolan mumbled. Iacane either didn't hear him or ignored him. "This is the man that's supposed to help us track down Ean?"

"He might have an idea. But we won't know until we get out of here first.

Come on."

Shay had followed Iacane outside and was staring at something. Her face crinkled with worry. When Ezzy maneuvered through the crumbling walls and got outside, she saw why.

A path of destruction ran directly in line with the building they were exiting out of through a number of other buildings in the village. Some houses had corners ripped off of them while others had similar holes going right through the middle. At least two homes had completely collapsed in on themselves.

"Ezzy..." Nolan whispered at her side.

"I know."

Paz. She had called for her construct to come to her and the thing had followed her simple order. In a daze at the time, she hadn't given the instruction to go around objects on its way. Paz had taken a straight line directly to her.

Ezzy felt like she had been struck in the gut. How many homes had she destroyed? Was anyone hurt? Maybe she should have Paz come and help her look for injured people in the rubble. Of course anyone that saw the destruction would most likely be scared to death of her Vilathos.

"Someone's coming."

Shay's voice brought Ezzy back to the present. Following the woman's gaze, Ezzy saw a woman wildly swinging her arms as she approached. A woman with braided auburn hair, chubby cheeks, wearing brown pants and a blacksmith's apron.

Syla Trane.

"You have to get out of here," the woman panted as she reached them. "Some of the villagers...urk!"

The woman cut off as Shayua grabbed her by the throat and lifted her into the air. The blacksmith beat at the arms of her captor, but even in her weakened condition Shayua was much stronger.

"Should I snap this traitor's neck now, Esmerelda?" The fact that Shay had used her full name told Ezzy that the woman wasn't bluffing. She really would kill her. Still able to see what scars and bruises Iacane hadn't been able to heal, Ezzy didn't blame her. But Ezzy needed to know why the woman had handed them over.

"Let her down. I want to hear what she has to say. It must be good for her to risk approaching us after what she did."

Shay frowned but did as she was asked. She kept a tight grip on the woman's neck though. Syla looked both relieved and guilty at the same time.

"Well?" Ezzy asked. "Speak. We aren't in a position to stand around here all day."

"They threatened me! Those Orange Hound people. Threatened to destroy my shop, take me away in chains, and sell me off. I was too scared to go to the Janpair family for help. They are a strange lot to begin with. For all I knew, the Orange Hounds had already paid them off."

"So, you betrayed us to save your own skin."

"What else could I have done? Your family doesn't have the power or influence anymore to protect me."

Ezzy wanted to lash out at the woman, but she knew Syla was right. That didn't pardon her for the betrayal though.

"Shay? What do you think? You've suffered the most because of this woman's actions."

"I believe her," Shay said, her face as unreadable as a wall. "This one isn't strong or skilled enough to defend herself from those men. If she was forced to betray us, I hold no ill will towards her for what happened."

"Well, you heard her," Ezzy said. "I guess we won't kill you. But I will expect you to help us clean up the mess..."

"That's why I came running to find you," the blacksmith cut in. "The villagers that witnessed your Vilathos's destruction have already headed up to the Janpair's estate. It's only a matter of time before they send their men after you. I don't know if you've met Bavian Toll, but the man is as ruthless as he is crazy. You have to get out of the village as quickly as possible."

"I'm not going to just leave when there might be people I've hurt--"

"Most of the villagers are out at their day jobs. You didn't hurt or injure anyone, but when they return, they will be looking for revenge. Things aren't handled here like they are in the other villages and Lurthalan. The Janpairs let mob justice handle most disputes that don't directly affect them. If the Janpair don't capture you first, the rest of the village will tear you apart. You have to go."

"But I could help rebuild the homes." Waving back at the building behind her. "It's not like the Orange Hound gang is going to be bothering us for a while."

"Esmerelda, you don't get it. The people that have lived here their entire lives are...off. I've seen them stone a man for trampling someone's flowers. You have to leave, at least until things calm down. Maybe in a few seasons you could come back and make reparations, but for now, you need to go."

"Ezzy," Nolan said, placing a hand on her shoulder. "As much as I want to take this woman to task for what she did to us, after spending only a short time here and seeing the people that live here, I'm leaning towards believing her."

"Nolan... I..."

Shay moved close and put a hand on Ezzy as well.

"As painful as it is, I agree with Nolan as well. If these people return looking for blood, things could get very ugly. How many people might die because I'm trying to defend us? Or how much worse could things get if you need to use your Vilathos to keep us safe? We could end up doing even more harm."

Ezzy looked at the needless destruction Paz had caused and her heart sank. This was different than what had happened in Wethrintir. What happened here was just carelessness on her part. Well, she would make amends. Maybe not today or anytime in the foreseeable future, but she would return and make things right. After she found Ean.

"Iacane, come here."

The man walked up, a smarmy smile painting his face.

"I don't think we've been introduced yet, although you seem to know--"

"Ean Sangrave."

"What? That's your name?"

"No, that's the name of the man I'm looking for. A man you've recently met on a trip to the Deadlands."

The smile disappeared, along with some of the color in the man's face.

"Um...the name sounds familiar. A lot of things happened on that trip. It was a horrible affair..."

"I don't have time for this, Iacane. My name is Esmerelda Ciantar. My father, Meganan, died on that trip because of the actions of Ean Sangrave. I want to find him, and I have it on good authority that you spent a good deal of time with him on the way to the Deadlands. If you know anything about where he is or where he came from, I want you to tell me. Now."

"Yes, ok, ok. Ean Sangrave. Young man, short black hair. Kind of awkward around other people. Yes I remember him and his sister. They were from Rottwealth, I believe."

"Fredren Prown didn't know the sister's name. What is it?

"Ah Fredren, ah-hem. Glad to hear that boy made it out alive--"

"Iacane..."

"Yes, sorry. Azalea is his sister. Cute lass, can hold her ale let me tell you. The two of them seemed strange, they certainly didn't act like brother and sister, but I wasn't about to call--"

"You said they came from Rottwealth? Are you sure?"

"Yes. It was mentioned once or twice. I don't think they would have any reason to lie to me."

Rottwealth. A backwater village, named for the rare healing herb that grew only within its borders. The temples had restricted travel to and from the village for decades without giving a reason. The ban had recently been lifted. Did that have anything to do with Ean?

It didn't matter. Elation began to smother out the guilt that had been weighing Ezzy down. She was getting closer. With any luck, Ean was there, hiding out because of what he had done. It would be the perfect place to hide. Even Ezzy hadn't considered it. Thoughts of finding justice for her father overpowered any last remaining feelings of guilt for what she had done here. Rottwealth was almost directly west of here. Leaving now, they could be there in about fourteen days.

"We're leaving."

"Excellent idea," Iacane said, nodding quickly. "I wish you the best of luck."

"You don't need to wish us luck. You're coming with us."

"But--"

Ezzy raised a hand to silence him, then turned to Shay.

"I need you to go back into the house, try to find our things, especially the key to our room at the inn. It's risky, but we can't leave without our supplies."

"I understand. I'll grab some of the discarded weapons just in case. We can always sell them for money if we don't have to use them." The woman jogged back into the house.

"Nolan, I want you to get started traveling. I'm going to have Paz carry you to help you get out of town. I'll follow my connection to wherever you are."

"Ezzy, I don't want to leave you here."

"We don't have time to argue, so I'm going to be blunt. You're slow. That leg of yours barely keeps you moving. I want you to get a good head start, especially if the rest of us need to get out of here fast."

"Yes, you're quite right, of course. I'll go."

"Good." Ezzy was surprised when Shay climbed back out of the house carrying a large sack. "Did you find our things already?"

"Yes, and I have four extra swords we can use to barter or sell."

"Excellent. Everyone move away from the house. I'm going to have Paz come out now."

When her companions had all moved away, she sent the command. The house groaned as Paz used the support beams off the floor to climb out of the hole. She watched through Paz's jeweled eyes as it pulled itself up onto the first floor and then make his way out of the house. Ezzy was shocked that the building remained standing.

Once Paz had reached them, she sent the mental command for it to follow Nolan, then went over and gave the man a hug.

"Be careful out there."

"You be careful here. You're the one taking the real risk. I'm just going for a walk."

"We can both agree to be careful. Now get going."

"Whatever you say, boss." He flashed her a grin and then started on his way, Paz a few steps behind him.

"Excuse me," Iacane said, rubbing his hands together. "I'm curious why you need me, besides the obvious fact that I'm the best Saniteal in the land."

"Well, for one, we might need you to go into the inn to get our things if it's being watched."

"I don't think I should be getting involved with--"

"Listen, Iacane. You're the only one I've found that has met Ean in person, so I need to keep you around for a while. Besides, if helping me isn't reason enough, think about this. Everyone in this godforsaken town thinks you're with us. Do you really want to stay behind to face the consequences for what happened alone?

Iacane shuffled about. A few times he opened his mouth to speak then it snapped shut again.

"Good, then it's settled. Quick stop to get our things and then we can get out of here."

"It will be good to leave this place," Shayua said, sniffing at the air.

"Agreed, Shay. We've been here long enough." The excitement Ezzy was feeling threatened to overwhelm her.

"It's time to resume our hunt."

TO BE CONTINUED...

<<<<>>>>

About the
Author

James R. Vernon was born and lives on the planet Earth. He holds a degree in education, which has zero influence on his writing. Instead he has spent as much free time as possible reading the works of both famous and not so well known authors to help improve on his own work. Often stuck in long commutes for his job James's imagination was free to create new worlds and stories. Through the assistance of family, friends, and some generous backers, James has been able to pursue his dream of sharing his stories with more then just the characters he has created. With the help of reliable beta readers and an excellent editor, James has been able to produce stories that have been able to entertain a few readers.

When not writing, he can usually be found with those he holds most dear, teaching those that put more white in his hair every year, losing money playing poker, losing time in a good book or song, or completely lost in the maze of his own mind.

Oh, and obviously he tries to enjoy life as much as he can.

For more information about James and the Three Moons Realm, visit us at

jamesrvernon.com !

Or on Facebook at
https://www.facebook.com/james.vernon.1694
and
https://www.facebook.com/threemoonsrealm

<<<<>>>>